COLD SECRETS

A SWAMP YANKEE MYSTERY

BOOK TWO

JAMES Y. BARTLETT

For information contact;

Yeoman House Books
10 Old Bulgarmarsh Road
Tiverton, RI 02878

www.jamesybartlett.com

Cover design by Todd Fitz of Fuel Media

ISBN: 978-1-7363930-4-8

First Edition: April 2022

Second Edition: February 2026

10 9 8 7 6 5 4 3 2 1

For Susan

"And above all, watch with glittering eyes the whole world around you because the greatest secrets are always hidden in the most unlikely places. Those who don't believe in magic will never find it."

-- *Roald Dahl*

CHAPTER 1

REVENGE IS A dish best served cold, as the old proverb says. Except, of course, there really isn't a proverb that says that, either in French or in English. I prefer Sir Francis Bacon's variation on the theme: "Revenge is a kind of wild justice."

As a former cop; as a former cop who served eight months at the Adult Correctional Institute, the fancy name for the Big House here in Rhode Island; as a former cop framed by the Attorney General for his own corrupt purposes; I was indeed interested in wild justice when I finally got freed. Any way I could get it.

It was that thirst for revenge—as overwhelming and all encompassing as if I had been marching across the desert for weeks without water— that pretty much dominated my life when I first regained my freedom. I awoke every morning, in my warm and comfortable bed, in my warm and comfortable house by the sea, in the company, usually, of my warm and comfortable partner Siggi … and could only think of the things I'd like to do to Preston Knox, the afore-mentioned attorney general, and some of the other players who sent me to prison and worked to keep me there. For no good reason other than to protect a beautiful young woman who was running a human trafficking ring right here in my hometown of Little Penwick, the smallest town in the smallest state. My anger and desire for revenge was Texas-sized, and not to be denied.

I was red hot and I would have gladly spooned into the mouth of Preston Knox some heaping servings of revenge *flambe* if I could. It was Siggi who kept me from doing anything rash and ridiculous in those first weeks of freedom.

"There's too much negative energy coming from you right now," she told me, usually after we had our morning coffee. The elapsed time from waking with a desire to kill someone to having downed a couple cups of joe was maybe half an hour, but despite the caffeine it helped me calm down, reduced the desire to commit mayhem back down to a more manageable level, where maybe some prudent maiming or a couple of painful broken limbs would have satiated my need for payback.

And I suppose my age and position in life helped as well. I was now retired after spending more than thirty-five years on the force of the Little Penwick Police Department, the last twenty-six as chief. My son Gus was now installed in my place as chief, which made me proud and happy. I hadn't decided what to do with the rest of my life, yet, although I knew I wasn't ready to decamp to Florida with the rest of the snowbirds and try to find happiness on a golf course or a sandy beach. But I figured I would find something useful after I had taken care of the revenge problem.

"It's not negative energy," I told Siggi, "It's pure, clean, 100-proof anger."

"You must do something to eliminate it," she would say. "It's not healthy to hold that inside you."

"OK," I said. "I will."

Of course, Siggi was thinking along the lines of doing some serious meditation, or Reiki massage or hot stone therapy or something. She is, in addition to being a part-time pediatric nurse, a practicing astrologer, and has been since she was a teenager. She learned the skill from her mother, who was Icelandic, having met and married an American G.I. during the second World War, when he was stationed in Reykjavik. Siggi had been born and grew up in the United States, but was still largely Nordic, a culture that gave us Odin, Thor and the reading of the Runes. She could do that, too, but was still mostly a student of the movements of the stars, the planets, the sun, and the moon, from which she could, quite accurately, determine the probabilities and proclivities of one's behavior and thus, the probabilities of future events.

I was a cop, so I was naturally skeptical of all such things. But as a cop, I had also observed how often Siggi's readings and projections turned out to come true. So I had learned to listen to her. You don't have to be an adherent of the skill to notice if it works or not.

But I was not thinking of therapy, whether New Age or Freudian, to assuage my white-hot rage. No, I was thinking of ways I could put a couple caps in the head of the sitting Attorney General of Rhode Island and watch the light slowly go out in his eyes. Thinking about that part was easy, and therapeutic in its own way. The hard part was coming up with a way to accomplish it while also avoid being sent back to the

ACI. Contemplating that aspect of my problem, turning it over and over in my head from the time I awoke until the moment I fell back asleep that night, that was what kept me going in those first few months after I got out. Whatever works, right?

So my … what? …recovery? … recuperation? … reentry into society? … took a while. It was the holidays when I first got out, so I pretty much laid low. Didn't go out much. Didn't have anyone come over, except for Siggi and my son, Gus. I sat at home and festered.

Towards the end of January, I took some baby steps. Called a few old friends and arranged for a weekly guys lunch at Jack's Diner. That was good: the guys listened to me, sympathized with my anger, told me it was understandable, based on what had happened. None of them believed what had happened to me was in any way justified. But none of them volunteered to help me murder Preston Knox and drop his body at the bottom of the Atlantic, way down deep in the trenches of that part of the ocean bottom they call The Dump. That made me a little angry, but I managed not to let it show. Siggi would have been proud.

In February, there was a get-together at Vera Phillip's place, where Gus is living in her garage apartment, to watch the Super Bowl. Siggi went with me, and Gus' honey, the Providence lawyer Maggie Wells, who had been installed as the Special Master by the AG to oversee the Little Penwick PD while I was in jail, was there as well.

We had a nice dinner and enjoyed watching the Patriots run up the score in the second half on the Bears. I listened as Gus and Maggie laughingly rehashed the Ferro case, which involved the beautiful young Glitter Girl, Janine Stone, who had devised and operated the trafficking scheme, and who had managed to escape arrest at the end. She was still on the loose.

But Gus and Maggie mentioned how a local judge, Mary-ann Parker, had tipped off Preston Knox when they had gone to get a search warrant from her for the Ferro place. As a result, the Ferro's had cleaned up their act and Janine had evaded our grasp again.

"Did you ever find out why she called Knox?" I asked.

Gus looked at me funny—I think he could feel the anger coming off me like waves of heat from a volcano—and said "They have been family friends for ages, Dad."

"You know what Rhode Island is like," Maggie said. "It's so small that it's almost incestuous. Everybody grew up with everybody else. And everybody knows everybody else's business."

"Yeah, but the judge endangered your investigation," I said. "Not only illegal, and totally unethical, but someone could have gotten hurt."

Siggi reached over and put her hand on top of mine. I got the message and let it drop.

But the next morning, first thing, I was on the phone. I called Gil James, an almost-retired reporter for the Newport *Daily News* in that small city across the Sakonnet River from Little Penwick. Gil, who had to be even older than me, had been reporting the goings-on around Newport seemingly forever, and the paper, now owned by a big national chain, had downsized almost everyone else on the staff. But they kept Gil around either because he knew where the bodies were buried or because the readers still liked to read his weekend column musing on the changes to the City by the Sea, and how much different, and better, things used to be.

"Chief Haddock," he said when I got him on the blower. "Or, ex-Chief I guess is more accurate. How is your boy doing?"

"Busy as hell," I said, "Arresting every miscreant he can get his hands on."

"Umm-hmm," Gil said. "If I remember the crime numbers from Little Penwick, that adds up to about three or four arrests a year. Am I right?"

"Pretty close," I said.

He chuckled. "So what can I do for you?"

"What's the dirt on Maryann Parker?" I asked.

"What makes you think our lovely local jurist has any dirt?" Gil asked, barely able to keep the sarcasm out of his voice.

"You can't get appointed judge in this state unless you've got some dirt hidden somewhere," I said. "I think it's a state law."

"Ain't that the truth," Gil said. "Let me see. Maryann Parker. Well, she's an old family friend of the attorney general."

"I know that," I said.

"The governor likes her. But then, the womenfolk tend to stick together."

"And who can blame them?" I said. "With menfolk like we have in this state lurking around out there."

"She's quite active at the Ida Lewis Yacht Club," he told me.

"She's a big sailor and keeps her boat at the club. She's been appointed Vice Admiral or whatever they call themselves."

"Lots of vice, is there, at the Ida Lewis?"

"Har-de-har," he said. "But I remember hearing that she got the club to approve paying for her anchorage fees. The way my source explained it, she did it on the QT. Didn't want the club membership to know about it, much less the general public. Guess she thought special favors for a sitting judge might not go down well with the voters."

"Must be a lot of money involved if she was trying to bury it," I said.

"About twenty-five hundred a year," Gil told me. "Most people who own yachts and keep them in Newport Harbor, twenty-five bills is pocket change. Petty cash."

"But for your average Joe Slobbo, that's a lot of cash," I said. "And her trying to keep it secret sounds like a cover-up."

"Not to mention the other members of the yacht club, each of whom has to pony up their mooring fees along with the membership dues every month—and it ain't cheap, believe me—they would not be happy that their Vice Admiral is getting a benny that they aren't."

"Interesting," I said. "I think I can use that. Thanks Gilly."

"Use it how?" As an old reporter, his ears had pricked up. Those old guys knew a story before it came up and slapped them across the face.

"Not sure yet," I said. "I'll let you know."

"You do that," he said.

ABOUT A WEEK later, Gil James called me back.

"You went to the Projo?" he said, his voice quivering with

indignation. "And the TV idiots? What are we, chopped liver?"

"Gil," I said, "You were the one who told me about Vice Admiral Maryann and her special deal. You could have run that story any time in the last five years. So don't go busting my chops."

He was silent. Because what I said was true.

He was referring to a big story in the Sunday Providence *Journal*—the Projo to us locals—which had been instantly aped by two of the three local TV stations in Providence. "Self-dealing on the Poop Deck" was the Projo's mostly nonsensical headline. They had gone with the narrative that the big, powerful, Superior Court justice had given herself a nice fat annual benefit and then tried to keep knowledge of it away from the other members of the yacht club. At least they had shown some reporting gumption and found three other yacht club members at the Ida Lewis to give them appropriately outraged quotes. Towards the end of the story, Judge Maryann Parker had been allowed to claim the $2500 annual credit she received, which was exactly the annual mooring fee members were charged, was typical for yacht clubs like Ida Lewis.

The TV stations had sent crews down to Newport to photograph the yacht club building, located on a small rock a few hundred yards out into the harbor, connected by a long wooden pier to the mainland. The eponymous Ida Lewis had once been a lighthouse keeper out on that rock in the 1800s, and rowed herself out to work every day, in between brave rowboat rescues of drunken sailors who fell into Newport Harbor from time to time. Nobody, from the judge herself to anyone from the yacht club, would go on camera, so the reporter just reiterated the Projo story over the images of the club, and the small handful of pleasure boats left on their moorings during the winter months.

"She's not going to resign because of this," Gil told me. "I called her husband last night. She's mad. She's embarrassed. But she's not quitting. No laws were broken. She just acted like an entitled yachty. Which, of course, she is."

"Good," I said. "All I wanted was to fire a shot across her bows. Mission accomplished."

"Geez," Gil James said over the phone. "What did she do to you? She wasn't the judge who sent you up the river. That was Freddie O'Rourke, wasn't it?"

"Maybe he's next," I said.

"Ho-lee crap," Gil said. "Remind me never to get on your bad side."

I FELT A little better after that, so I began doing some much-needed repairs and maintenance on my house. Of course, I didn't have a chance to work on the house when I was jailed. And before that, the demands of the job at the police department often left me little time for the small jobs one needs to keep up with at home.

They were mostly small jobs because the house was in pretty good shape. My grandfather, John Edward Haddock, had built the place himself, back around 1930. John Edward had been a merchant marine captain and he found the sliver of land that was a rocky meadow overlooking the shingle beach down below, with a view out across the Rockies, a collection of moss- and lichen-covered outcroppings just offshore. They were pretty to look at, when they weren't being battered and beaten by the wind and tides and occasional storms. The views were great, but everyone in Little Penwick tried to tell John Edward that the lot he chose was probably the most inhospitable lot in town. Underneath, it was all rock and shale. On the surface, the constant winds, the frequent howling winter gales, the lashing rain and snow made it likely that no structure would last very long. And even if it did, they all told John Edward, the cost of heating the place in the winter would be prohibitive.

But John Edward was an ornery old cuss who did things his own way. And in building his house, he went about it without care or concern of what other people might think, or even worrying about the way other people built their homes.

In his voyages up and down the Eastern seaboard, John Edward had gotten to know timber men in Maine, the Canadian provinces and even down South. So he knew who made the strongest beams and best boards, and he paid a little extra to have that shipped down to Little Penwick. He dug out his own basement, mostly by hand, with a little mechanical help once he hit the shale, which wasn't that far down. He mixed his own concrete in a medium-size drum mixer, using both the sand and the pebbles he hauled up from the beach below. The roof was double-laid with plywood bolted to the support beams for extra strength. Every part of the house was thickly insulated and the inside was paneled with Southern cypress, noted for its strength as well as its honey-colored beauty. And he made up the architecture as he went. It was mostly a one-story structure with kitchen, living room, dining room and master bedroom and bath all on one level. He added two small bedrooms for kids—who didn't yet exist—over the garage. Then he added a deck outside, to take advantage of those nice views of the ocean.

Despite the naysayers, it all worked. And now I lived here, in a house that was still on the small side, but was as solid as granite, warm, cozy, draft-free and which had lasted all these decades without incident. Turned out John Edward Haddock had known what he was doing and everyone else in town did not.

So I spent the next few weeks working on some of the small to-do items that had built up. Re-roofed the garage. Built a couple more raised-bed planters for Siggi to use to grow veggies in the summer. Trucked in some new crushed oyster shells to line the driveway. Started replacing some of the worn deck boards and added a new coat of stain.

I thought I was doing fairly well. My white-hot rage had cooled a little, and I was able to think about other things, now and then. Preston Knox was not foremost in my mind. But Siggi saw something else. She looked at me one morning over a cup of coffee and said "You need to get going, Julius."

"Going where?" I asked.

"On your life journey," she said. "Jupiter is moving direct into your House of Enterprise. This is a very powerful time and that means you need to get moving."

"Where am I supposed to go?"

She smiled. Then she got up, walked over to my pass-through counter, and picked up a white envelope that had been sitting there, untouched, for months. She came back and put it down in front of me.

"Maybe start there," she said.

I looked at the envelope. It was from some state licensing board up in Providence and it contained my approved application to be a private investigator in the state of Rhode Island. I had actually made the application when I was still Inmate #GH37-3290. They sent it back to me—approved—just before I was released. The all-knowing, all-seeing state bureaucracy can be pretty dense.

"You need clients to start a business," I said. "I don't have any of those."

"I think the way it works is, you start a business and then begin to prospect for clients," she said. "You have to take the first step first."

"What I really want to do is investigate that bastard Knox," I said. "And then take him out into the swamps and break some of his most important bones."

Siggi sighed. She had heard this before. "I understand your need for revenge," she said. "I feel it, too, quite often. But there are good ways, and not so good ways to get what you want."

"What are the so-called good ways?"

"The best way is for you to become a productive member of society again," she said. "He tried to take that away from you. Only you can put it back. Better, this time. That will show that man that he failed."

I got up and poured myself another cup of coffee.

"And you think this is the way to do it?' I said, nodding at the envelope with my new PI license.

"I think it's a start," she said. "And you'll never get any-where unless you start someplace."

"Aren't we the Adage Factory this morning?" I said.

She laughed.

"You mentioned a few weeks ago that there were some old cases that had never been closed," she said.

"Cold cases," I said. "Yeah, we had a few at the depart-ment. Every police department has a couple. About once a year, we'd drag them out of storage and take another look at them. See if anything jumps out. Or if we might have missed something important."

"Why don't you pick one of those and give it a deep dive?" she said. "It would be police work of a sort. And you might surprise yourself and find something."

I sipped my coffee while I thought about that. It wasn't a bad idea.

"And while you're working on that, you can see if you pick up any other cases or clients," she said. "I think once the word gets out that Julius Haddock is up and about again, you'll have more cases than you can handle."

"Your lips to God's ears," I said. "Of course, all that won't help me destroy Preston Knox."

She shook her head. "There's that negative energy again," she said. "I think you need to focus on more positive things, like helping review those cold cases and then assisting people with their problems. Perhaps it's best to leave Preston Knox to the universe. Most of the time, bad people get what's coming to them."

"That's kind of the policeman's adage," I said with a smile.

She smiled back. "Do you have any idea of which cold case you'd want to take up first?" she asked.

I nodded. "Yeah, the oldest one," I said. "The Dixon case."

"Then do it," she said. "Couldn't be a better time to launch a new venture."

CHAPTER 2

It was a lovely sunny day for early April, so that morning I applied a coat of stain to the decking outside my back door. And after lunch I drove over to the Little Penwick Police Station, around the corner from the village green.

I went inside the police half of the Public Safety building—the Fire Department occupied the other half—and nodded at Jerry Hanlon, who was the officer on duty at the front desk. I walked on into the open squad room, with its four metal desks scattered with papers, notepads, telephone message slips, binders and folders, all as messy and seemingly chaotic as ever, and went back to the office of Jessica Martin. Jessica had been promoted to Lieutenant Commander after New Year's, replacing Barry Callahan, who had retired. Jessica was in her mid-forties now, still fit and slim, but with that mid-age air of competence and knowledge. She'd been around the block more than a few times, and carried herself with the confidence that there was very little she could not handle.

Her face lit up when she saw me.

"Chief!" she said, bounding up out of her desk chair and coming around to give me a big hug and a kiss on the cheek. "How are you doing? What a nice surprise!"

"Hiya, L.C.," I said, "Thought I'd better stop by and make sure you weren't screwing up the police organization I spent my lifetime building."

"Ha-ha," she fake-laughed. "If we're screwing up, it's all the fault of your boy Gus, not me!"

I laughed. "True," I said. "And I probably can't blame him, since everything he learned was from me in the first place."

"What brings you in to see us?" she asked.

"I'm looking for the files on the Dixon case," I said. "Are they still here in this building?"

"That old case?" she said, eyebrows raised in surprise. "Geez, that was a few years ago, wasn't it?"

"1991," I said. "Summer of."

"What do you want with that stuff?" she asked. "Probably has half an inch of dust on it."

"I'm gonna make another pass at it," I said. "Use my time fruitfully. Plus, I got a brand new PI license and I thought I'd take it out for a spin."

She nodded. "Not a bad idea," she said. "Nobody else will ever give a damn about that case. It is as cold as a snowball in February."

"Yeah," I said. "I know. That's why I thought maybe a new pair of eyes, another look. You never know."

She went back behind her desk and punched some keys on her computer, frowning in concentration. She waited, watching, then nodded.

"Yeah," she said. "Says here we got the box on that case up in the storage space." She wrote something down on a Post-It note and handed it to me. Then she fished around in her desk drawer and came out with a set of keys, which she also handed to me. "I haven't been up there in a couple of years. That gives you the last known shelf location for the file box. But it's fifty-fifty if you'll find it there. If not, just look around. It's supposed to be up there somewhere."

"Great," I said, "I'll go up and take a look. Thanks, kid."

"No problem," she said. Then she paused and looked at me. "Gus is OK with this, right?"

I winked at her. "Natch," I said. I gave her a wave and headed for the stairs at the back of the building. Of course, my son had no idea what I was planning to do, but I was pretty sure he wouldn't object.

The storage space was on the third floor. It was really floor two-and-a-half, tucked under the sloping roof. There were about six rows of metal shelves, filled to overflowing with file boxes and other containers filled with evidence from past cases. I flipped on the lights and went looking for the row indicated on the Post-It note. It was on the last shelf, at the back. A large legal-sized storage box with a taped-on lid. It was labeled in black marker: Dixon, Donna. 1991.

"Bingo," I said. I carried the box over to a metal table in the center of the space and, with my pocket knife, I slit open the tape holding the top on the box, lifted it away and looked inside.

The box was three-quarters full of file folders and three-ring binders. There were no plastic bags holding evidence, like clothing or weapons or items that had been fingerprinted. Just lots of paper. That was not surprising to me at all. There had never been much evidence in the Donna Dixon case. That was one main reason why it was still cold, after thirty years.

I pulled a couple of the files out and glanced through them. Then I started packing it all back in again.

"Okay," said a voice from behind me. "Up against the wall and spread 'em. Interfering with police business."

I finished putting the last files back in the box, set the lid in place and turned around to face my son, Gus Haddock, the current chief of police.

"Hey, Junior," I said. "What's up?"

"The usual," he said. "Jess told me you were up here looking for an old file. Which one?"

I pointed at the box on the table. "Dixon case," I said, "1991. Thirty years ago."

Gus looked confused.

"Teen aged girl," I said. "Riding to work on her bike. Disappeared, We found her body the next morning."

He shrugged. "Way before my time," he said. "Never heard of it."

I nodded. "That's why it's still cold, after all these years. Whoever did it left nothing behind. No finger prints, no DNA, no nothing."

Gus nodded, folding his arms across his chest. Even in just the year or so that he had been back in town, after serving three tours with the Army Rangers over in the Mideast, I could see that he had settled into his new job. He looked rested and relaxed, at ease in his skin. If ever there had been someone born to a job, it was Gus Haddock and the job of chief of the Little Penwick PD. And it wasn't because I had held that job while he was growing up, although that helped Junior learn how police departments operate. But that combined with his own experience as a Ranger officer, the wartime experiences he had, had crafted him into a solid, dependable, no-nonsense, highly effective leader.

"And why are you taking away the case files?" he asked.

"I'm going to take another look at it," I said. "See if any of us missed anything thirty years ago."

"Were you involved with that case?" he asked.

I shook my head. "Not really," I said. "I was on the force when that happened, but I was just a patrolman. Had no hand in the investigation. Other people did that. Which is why I thought taking a new look might be interesting."

He looked at me. I saw a shadow fall across his face.

"Ah, Dad," he said, hesitating. "You're not officially part of the department any more."

"Geez," I said, "How did my own son get to be such a brilliant investigator? I mean, no shit Sherlock."

He held out his hands in protest. "Now, don't go getting all hot around the collar," he said. "I mean, I just want to make sure that we're on the same page here."

"You got a problem with me looking at this case?"

"No," he said, "Of course not."

"You just want to remind me that when I find out who killed Donna Dixon thirty years ago, that I can't arrest the guy," I said. "I gotta call you to do that, right?"

"Well, yeah," he said, his face reddening. "But that's not what I meant…"

"Then spit it out, Junior," I said. "I'm a man. I can take it."

"Now, Dad," he said, "Don't be that way. I'm just concerned about you running around all over town grilling people about something that happened 30 years ago. There might be some people in town who'd think that was a little … umm … strange."

"Strange," I said. I let that word sit there in the air for a moment. "We might be able to catch a killer after 30 years, assuming he's still alive to be caught. But you're worried about people feeling strange."

"No, that's not what I meant," he said, stumbling a little.

"Look, Junior," I said. "Here's the deal. Siggi thinks I need to get my House of Accomplishments into gear. I have my new PI license. And, after twenty-six years running this department, I think I understand police procedure pretty well. And most of the people in this town know who I am and what I'm all about. So nobody will think it strange if I take a look at this case and maybe ask a few questions. Okay? We good?"

"Long as you keep me posted, we're good," he said.

"Right," I said. I picked up the big box and started out the door with it.

"Don't forget to sign a chain of evidence form with Jessica," he called after me.

Both my hands were occupied in carrying the box, so I couldn't show him my perfectly matched set of middle fingers.

"Lock the door when you leave," I called out over my shoulder as I headed down the stairs.

CHAPTER 3

THE NEXT DAY dawned sunny and even warmer than the day before. The feel of spring was noticeable in the air, that humid warmth combined with the fecund smell of the earth coming alive, unfreezing, the seedlings and bulbs beginning their annual leap to life. But I had watched the eleven o'clock news the night before and heard the weatherman warning about a possible coastal storm that was heading up the East Coast and threatening to dump a half foot of wet, sticky snow on Little Penwick at the weekend. That was typical for a New England spring: one step forward, followed by snow.

Siggi had gone home to her own place after dinner the night before, so I padded around the house doing not much. I looked at the big legal box on my dining table, but decided to hold off until I was ready to dive in. It was Wednesday, and that meant it was a Jack's day, so I got dressed and headed out for lunch a little before noon.

Jack's is the undistinguished name given to an undistinguished shack located over in Burr's Village. This was a tiny settlement inside the town of Little Penwick that dated back to Colonial times, over near the eastern border between Little Penwick and the town of Westport, Mass., where a couple of ancient roadways intersected. The tradition in Little Penwick was that then-Senator Aaron Burr of New York, campaigning for the Democrat-Republican Party of Thomas Jefferson in the presidential election of 1796, four years before Burr was named Vice President to Jefferson by the Congress, had come to Little Penwick and made a speech. Nobody remembered what Burr had said, just that he had made his address from the back of a wagon in this little settlement which was then renamed in his honor. Burr's Village had remained a backwater ever since, significant only for an old general store that had been in continuous business since about 1788 and the claim that the first of the breed of chicken known as Rhode Island Red had been developed on a nearby farm.

There was an old mill race next to the general store fed by a smallish pond. Jack's tiny wooden shack sat above the pond. I climbed the stairs and glanced over to check the water level in the pond. The town had been forced to make some repairs to the dam and the ancient waterworks some years earlier. The town council hadn't wanted to spend the money, but felt the only alternative was letting the pond drain away and most people in town felt that was unacceptable. Today, the pond was full, as there had been several days of rain in the last few weeks.

Jack's was a one-story building with a sharp pitched roof, clad in aging clapboards that badly needed a new coat of paint. The stairs groaned as I climbed up and the hinges on the front door squealed in outrage when I went through. Jack's was the antithesis of a modern new restaurant, which was why my friends and I—all of a certain age—liked to come here, at least once a week, for beer, lunch and catching up on the town gossip.

Inside, Junior Hastings, the current proprietor, the founding Jack being long since dead, sat in his place at the far end of the wooden bar that extended across the width of the shack. There were a few booths and tables in the front room and the kitchen was out back. Junior had a newspaper open in front of him and was dressed in his usual: denim bib overalls over a red checked flannel shirt. He nodded at me in greeting, and I went over to the stainless steel cooler behind the bar, reached in and helped myself to a cold bottle of Budweiser, snapped the top off on the opener affixed to the cooler and took it over to the round table in front of a window that overlooked the mill pond outside. My three friends were already there, each nursing his own bottle of beer.

"Hey Chief," said Billy Church, sitting at the far left of the table. "Nice out today, ain't it?" Church was a heavy-set man with a barrel chest, small bald head and beady eyes that peered out from behind thick glasses. He had been in the insurance business, taking over from his father and letting his daughter run the place now.

"Very nice," I said, pulling up a chair and joining the rest. "But I don't like what I'm hearing about the weekend."

"Cross that bridge when we get to it," mumbled Harlan Bailey, sitting next to Billy Church. "They say it may swing east and miss us altogether." Bailey ran an auto repair shop in Little Penwick, but had managed to get the school bus contract several decades ago, and that work had helped him keep his head above water in lean times. He was a thin and wiry man with stringy hair atop his small round head.

"Your lips to God's ears," I nodded. "I thought I'd shoveled the last snow for the season two weeks ago."

"You shouldn't be shoveling snow at your age," said Ben Almy, the last of the fearsome threesome at the table. Ben was some kind of engineer who had worked in the big defense contractor's plant over in Middletown. Exactly what it was he had engineered there nobody really knew, and he was not allowed to tell us, since it was probably something that was designed to explode and kill thousands of people. He looked like an engineer: a skinny, bony body that looked like it had been sitting at a desk for twenty years, flabby arms and a mostly bald head. "You'll have a coronary infarction and poor Siggi will come upon your frozen bod in a drift."

"Be the first time he's been stiff in twenty years," said Billy with a guffaw.

The others groaned. We started a conversation on the Red Sox, who had just opened their season with two losses to the Baltimore Orioles. None of us had high hopes for the team this season, but that was pretty much the default position every year. Most people of the vintage of the Jack's Wednesday crowd had grown old watching the Red Sox lose, year after year. It had only been in the 21st century that the organization had actually transformed itself into one of the American League's most powerful teams. But old timer Red Sox fans like us, weaned on endless seasons of constant loss and defeat, never trusted the team until they demonstrated that they could still pitch, hit and throw.

Meanwhile, Junior got off his bar stool at the end of the bar, went into the kitchen in the back and came out with a tray. There were mugs of hot chowder, plates with sandwiches and chips, and a basket filled with fresh-baked brownies. We all made various grunting sounds of pleasure and began to eat.

As we finished, we each got up and went over behind the bar and poured ourselves a cup of coffee from the Bunn drip machine there. Harlan sniffed his cup suspiciously.

"Yum," he said, "made fresh four hours ago."

Billy Church laughed. "You forget where you are," he said. "This is Jack's, the home of the hours-old coffee."

Junior Hastings looked over at them from behind the bar and frowned, but said nothing. He was not an argumentative sort, and likely figured if his customers didn't like the food, the coffee or the ambiance, they could just go somewhere else.

Back at the table, we passed around the brownies and sipped our coffee. Only Ben Almy passed on dessert. "Helen is worried about my weight," he said, patting his not unsubstantial belly. "She's convinced I'm gonna come down with the diabetes or something."

"So have a brownie," Billy Church said. "It'll speed things along, she'll be right and then you can croak."

"You guys seemed obsessed with death today," I said, cupping my coffee mug in my hands. "I'm gonna die in a snowbank and Bennie here is gonna blow his sugar stack or something. C'mon...it's springtime. The season of new life."

"Okay preacher," Billy responded. "What life-giving topic of conversation do you have for us?"

I paused for a beat or two, letting the coffee warm my hands.

"I'm going back to work," I said.

The other three looked at me like I had just announced I was planning on growing a second head.

"Are you out of your mind?" Ben Almy said. "At your age?"

Harlan Bailey looked at me, startled. "Are you taking over your old job? Gus isn't leaving town already is he?"

I laughed at the reaction. "Naw, I'm not going back to the department. That's a young man's game, and Junior has it under control," I said. "I've got a private investigator's license from the state. I'm planning on looking into some old cases and see if I find anything that was missed first time around."

They all thought about that for a while.

"Shit," said Billy Church, "I never paid a traffic ticket back in '87. The town never came after me for it. I'll bet I owe a couple thousand on it, with interest and penalties and all. Say, Julius, if I slip you a C-note, will you agree to just forget about it?"

They all laughed.

"You should slip me a C-note just on general principles," I said. "But I'm going after more serious cases. And not just ones here in Little Penwick. I'll bet there are some good cases collecting dust over on Aquidneck and down in Newport. Somebody ought to take a look, and I guess I'm just the guy to do that. Especially now that I have the time and interest."

That caused nodding around the table.

"I remember one," Harlan said. "That girl they found in the field, was on her way to work at the Kennedy farm stand. What was her name?"

"Donna Dixon," I said, nodding at Harlan. "That's the first one on my list. I've already pulled the files on it. I remember when it happened. I was fairly new on the force at the time."

"Remind me," Billy Church said. "I don't remember it at all."

"Seventeen year old girl," I said. "Had a summer job at the farm stand, keeping the corn table stacked and running the cash register. She came from a big family over near The Swamp, four or five siblings. On that day, nobody was able to give her a ride to work, so she decided to ride her bike. She'd done that before, so it was no big deal. But she never showed up for work. We found her body the next morning, at the edge of the Kennedy farm orchard, just off Main Road."

"Oh, I remember now," Billy said, nodding. "She was naked as a jaybird, right?"

"That's the one," I said. "But the medical examiner said she had not been sexually abused. Which was just one of the many odd things about that case. I mean, why would her killer strip her clothes off?"

"So you'd go chasing after all the sexual deviants in Little Penwick," Harlan said. "You know, like Ben Almy here. I heard he likes goats."

Ben flipped Harlan a bird. But he turned to look at me. "They never found who did it?" he asked.

I shook my head. "Nope. Never got even the first hint of a lead. Hell, the family, after about five years had passed, even brought in some psychics, hoping they could see the auras and emanations that would lead to the killer. As you'd expect, that turned out to be a total waste of time, except maybe for the psychics, who I assume got paid."

"And you think that now, thirty odd years later, you can find something?" Billy Church said, eyebrows raised.

"Don't know," I said. "But I have the time and the interest to jump in and look around. You never know."

"Okay, Marlowe," Harlan said. "We wish you luck. Sounds like you're gonna need it."

CHAPTER 4

I GOT HOME from Jack's in mid-afternoon and decided it was time. I was as ready as I was ever going to be.

I took the lid off the box on my dining table and began to lift out the stuff inside, making stacks according to relevance as I worked. At the front of the box was the Bible, the murder book, a three-ring binder covered in navy-colored plastic which contained the step-by-step documentation of the murder investigation into Donna Dixon's death. After that came stacks of other bound reports and files. The state Medical Examiner's post-mortem report was in the stack, and another folder contained the photographs that had been taken at the scene where her body had been found.

Once the contents of the case had been unpacked and put into my rough organization, I took a deep breath, opened the murder book and began to read.

The facts of the case, summarized at the beginning, were about as I remembered. Donna Dixon, age 17, had left her house late in the morning of June 25th to ride her bike to work at the Kennedy Farm roadside retail store. She had a summer job as a general assistant at the farm stand, which sold the produce from the 40-acre orchard, corn fields and vegetable patches. The farm and stand were owned and operated by Bob Kennedy and his wife Lucy.

Two of Donna Dixon's four siblings were at home with her mother when she left for work: fifteen year old Billy Dixon and twelve year old Franny. Donna had two older sibs as well: John, age 21 and Catherine, 23. John still lived at home but was at work at a furniture factory in Fall River, Mass., where he assembled office furniture, desks, file cabinets and tables. Cathy had moved out, to an apartment in Providence, where she worked as a sales clerk in a department store downtown.

Donna Dixon's father, Harold, was an English teacher at Portsmouth High School on Aquidneck Island, across the Sakonnet River from Little Penwick. He had been teaching a summer school class on the day she disappeared. The girl's mother, Betty, was a home-maker who did not work outside the home.

The Dixon family lived in a 1970s-era two-story on a circular street called Orchard Heights Road. There were twelve other houses on the street. To get to her workplace on her bike, Donna had two choices of route: she could have left Orchard Heights, ridden west on Swamp Road, a narrow lane through a forested part of Little Penwick which ended at Main Road, and then turned right or north on Main for a couple miles until she reached the farm stand.

Alternatively, she could have come out of Orchard Heights, turned left and then left again on Commons Road which would have taken her to the village green in the center of Little Penwick. From there, she could have peddled down Meetinghouse Lane over to Main Road and then north. It was roughly the same distance, no matter which route she had taken. The Swamp Road choice would have had less traffic, at least until she got to Main. Riding through the village green made it more likely she'd have been seen by someone along the way.

But no witnesses came forward to say they had seen a girl riding her bike that day, either along Swamp Road or in the center of town. Police interviews had turned up one woman who said she had seen a girl on a bike near the village green that morning, but she could not provide a description. It later turned out that a younger child had also been riding a bike near the elementary school that morning, so that might have been who the witness had seen.

In any case, Donna Dixon never made it work that day. She was scheduled to begin her shift at noon. When she hadn't appeared by one, the manager, Lucy Kennedy, called Donna's home and spoke to Betty Dixon, the girl's mother. Betty sent the two younger kids out to look for Donna, but they came back after riding their bikes around the neighborhood and into the center of town, and told their mother that they had seen no sign of their sister. When Donna still hadn't reported for work at three in the afternoon, Betty Dixon called her husband, who was about to head home for the day, his classes dismissed. Harold Dixon stopped by the farm stand on his way home and spoke to Lucy, then spent an hour driving around Little Penwick, looking for a girl on a bike.

In the meantime, Betty Dixon had called the home of Charley Stine, Donna's high school boyfriend. Betty spoke to Charley's mother, who said her son was spending the day at the beach with some buddies. That alibi checked out—the group of teen boys, six of them including Charley, had been hanging out at Gooseneck Beach, listening to the radio and doing not much of anything all day long. The police later talked with both women, for the record. There was one note that said the conversation between the mothers had ended with some angry words.

At six o'clock, Harold called the Little Penwick police and reported his daughter missing. The chief of police at that time, Roger Worrell, put out a bulletin to his department, which included a young patrolman named Julius Haddock, and told them to be on the lookout for the girl. But that was all he did at the time. Kids went missing from home a lot, usually to hang out with friends, sneak away with a sexual partner, go into the woods to smoke some weed, or just forget to call home to check in. Sometimes they ran away, heading for Providence, Boston or New York, looking for adventure or a new start in life. Nobody, at the time, thought Donna's disappearance was that big a deal. This was Little Penwick, a place where the worst sort of crime was usually speeding.

But at ten o'clock that night, with no word from Donna or anyone who had seen her all day, Chief Worrell had kicked it up a notch. He faxed out a statewide alert, asking all police departments in the state to be on the alert for the missing girl. Worrell sent one of his officers over to Orchard Heights to get a recent photograph of Donna, and when they had that, they sent it out on the statewide wire.

In the morning, Worrell elevated Donna's case to priority one. The morning shift, which had included the young Julius Haddock, was told to start looking in out-of-the-way places around town, and that violence could not be ruled out. Reading this part of the case record again, I remembered the jolt of adrenaline that I had felt that day. A girl gone missing overnight was something entirely unexpected in Little Penwick. All of us wondered if she was still alive, wondered if we were looking for a live girl or a dead body.

But I didn't find Donna Dixon. That fell to one of my colleagues, an officer named Roger Hart. Driving down Main Road, a few hundred yards south of the Kennedy farm stand, Hart had caught a glimpse of a metallic glimmer from the end of the orchard behind one of the ancient stone walls that delineate the pastures and fields of the Kennedy farm. Hart had stopped his squad car, and walked over to the stone wall, looking down between the rows of apple trees. He saw the handlebars of a bicycle lying in the grass beneath a tree. He went back to his squad car, called in the sighting and then clambered over the wall and walked down into the orchard.

That's where he found Donna Dixon. She was lying on the ground, on her back, naked save for one white sock on her left foot. Her arms were thrown out wide, her head turned to the right, eyes tightly closed. There appeared to be discolorations on her neck. Hart checked her pulse, There was none. He noted that her skin was cold. She was very, very dead.

Officer Hart stayed near the body until the other cars began arriving. They had set up a perimeter with yellow police tape, erected a screen around the body and the chief of detectives, Rick Schuster, began taking photographs. Chief Worrell, who also showed up at the scene, immediately called in the state police and the state crime lab technicians. They eventually arrived and also began carefully sifting through the crime scene and surrounding area looking for evidence. There was very little to find. It was speculated by those at the scene that the girl had been killed elsewhere and her body had been dumped in the orchard, post-mortem.

I GOT UP and walked outside to get some fresh air and to think a little about what I had just read. So far, the description of the case was pretty straightforward. Nothing I read jumped out at me as out of the ordinary. The girl had been stopped somewhere on her way to work, abducted, taken somewhere by her abductor, killed, and then her body had been transported to the orchard and dumped. That kind of timeline was not unusual for a murder of this kind. What was unusual was the lack of any witness at any part of the timeline. Nobody reported seeing Donna Dixon riding her bike, being stopped by anyone, and nobody reported seeing her body taken into the orchard to be dumped. Likewise, there was no physical evidence of any kind that would help point police in one direction or another. I looked out at the Rockies, awash in the afternoon sun and smelled the briny air. Then I went back inside and continued reading.

DONNA DIXON'S BODY had been taken to the state medical examiner's office on Orms Street next to the state capitol building in Providence. An autopsy had been performed by the chief medical examiner for the state, Dr. Sturmer, and his report, issued a few days later, stated that Donna Dixon had died from asphyxia due to strangulation. The report noted the presence of petechiae, or tiny hemorrhages in the eyes and skin due to the loss of oxygen, typical in a strangulation death. Her hyoid bone had been fractured. There was some bruising of the skin on her neck, consistent with the theory that she had been strangled by someone choking her with their hands.

The medical examiner noted that manual strangulation does not always result in the breaking of the hyoid, and that the cases in which it does occur are usually in older persons. His conclusion was that whoever strangled Donna Dixon had used excessive force. The ME therefore concluded that the perpetrator was likely a man.

Although the victim had been found without clothing, save for one sock, the report stated that Donna Dixon, although not a virgin, had not had recent sexual intercourse. Analysis of the one sock was inconclusive: there were no bodily fluids, strange fibers or anything else detected. The rest of the victim's clothing had never been found.

The ME's report also noted the absence of dew on the body that, as his report specified, would have been expected if the body had been placed in the orchard overnight, before dawn. Instead, the body had been dry and without the kinds of insect presence that might be expected if the body had been lying there for several hours. The ME's conclusion was that the victim had been left in the field either after dawn or shortly before dawn.

The internal temperature of the girl's liver had led the medical examiner to conclude she had been killed sometime around midnight the night before her body had been discovered.

After examining the girl's bicycle, no fingerprints, other than the victim's, had been found.

The rest of the girl's body was free of bodily fluids, fibers, trace materials…anything that could be used to link to a perpetrator or to a location where the crime had been committed.

STRANGLED, I THOUGHT to myself. *Likely by a man. With great force. Enough to break the girl's hyoid which, at age 17, was still flexible and strong. That indicated anger. Or some kind of extraordinary psychosis. Overcome by whatever demon had taken possession of him, the perp had, quite simply, choked the life out of her. What had triggered that kind of blind and powerful rage? Apparently not lust, as she had been untouched in that way. And the killer had not left behind any calling cards … semen or blood or saliva. He had just killed her, taken her body and her bicycle to the apple orchard early the next morning and dropped it off.*

I CLOSED THE cover of the murder book. I felt a little sick, down deep in my guts. It was unusual to have a case where the killer left nothing behind. In most cases, there was something, something for the investigators to latch onto and probe. A strange fiber of some kind, a partial print, a witness who thought they had seen something. But not here. Donna Dixon had left home a bright young teenager with all her life ahead

of her, and then had just disappeared for several hours before turning up dead and naked in the Kennedy orchard. And
where would one begin to search for her killer? He had left
behind a blank slate. He was either very lucky, or very good.

CHAPTER 5

Superior Court Judge Frederick O'Rourke was a creature of habit. Part of his adherence to a certain unchanging routine was due to his age. Now 82, the Judge figured he didn't have anything left to prove to anyone else, so he did what he wanted. But there was also some degree of comfort in doing the same things, over and over, day after day. It was, in a way, reassuring.

Which was why Judge O'Rourke scheduled his hearings for the mornings. He showed up in court every day at nine a.m. sharp. The bailiffs and court reporters knew that they could set their watches by him. When the big hand hit the twelve and the little hand was on the nine, you could peek into Freddie O'Rourke's elaborately paneled courtroom on the fifth floor of the Licht Judicial Complex on Benefit Street in downtown Providence and watch as the door behind the raised bench opened, and the tiny white-haired old man dressed in his black robes came out of his chamber and took his seat.

After hearing whatever cases were on his schedule that day, he would glance at his watch sometime between noon and twelve-thirty, nod to himself and gavel the proceedings to a halt. The casual onlooker might assume that the judge was calling for the day's lunch break, which was partly true. But Freddie O'Rourke hated afternoon sessions. With a passion. So unless the case at hand demanded some kind of immediate attention, the lunch break would actually extend until nine a.m. the next morning.

No other judge on the bench could get away with three-hour workdays. But Freddie's advanced age and long years of service had earned him this quirk, and the Chief Judge of the Superior Court had given O'Rourke senior status and only assigned him cases that could be quickly handled, in most cases before the lunchtime deadline.

Out-of-state attorneys who came to argue some of the corporate cases that Judge O'Rourke often handled, were amazed at this situation. *That's Rhode Island*, they would be told. *That's the way we do things here.*

After the day's court session ended, Judge O'Rourke would finish up with his clerk, bid everyone a good day and walk across Benefit Street to Six Benevolent Street to the welcoming environs of The Hope Club where he would take his lunch in the Grill Room. His table would be waiting for him and as soon as he sat down, a waiter would bring him a martini with two olives. He would pretend to read the menu and then order the usual: the shepherd's pie with braised lamb and short ribs and mashed potatoes.

Unlike the other tables in the room, which were full of downtown businessmen, professors from nearby Brown University and other judges and lawyers from the courthouse across the street, Freddie O'Rourke preferred to eat alone. His table never was set with two places. He ate his lunch, drank his martini, patted his lips with his linen napkin and got up. He would nod at his waiter, nod at the maitre'd, nod at the girl behind the desk at the front of the club, and walk back across the street to the courthouse, take the elevator down to the garage, get his car and drive the 1.25 miles to his mansion on one of the side streets off Grotto Road, east of Blackstone Boulevard, up on the hill above Bailey's Cove in the Seekonk River.

But today, his schedule was interrupted. When Freddie O'Rourke drove up Blackstone, a Providence police cruiser came up behind him, flashed the blue lights and the officer hit the squelch siren a couple times. Freddie O'Rourke pulled over.

The officer came to his driver's window.

Freddie was ready, handing him his driver's license. It was inside a leather holder than also happened to have O'Rourke's judicial ID on the other side. The officer glanced at the documents and nodded.

"Afternoon Judge," he said. "Can I ask you to get out of the vehicle, please?"

"What's the problem, officer?" O'Rourke said.

"Please just exit the vehicle for me, sir," the officer said.

Cursing under his breath, but not far enough under that the officer didn't hear it, Freddie O'Rourke turned off his car, put it in park and got out. Slowly, as any 82-year-old would.

"Please stand on the sidewalk over there, sir," the officer said, motioning to the side of Blackstone Boulevard. Here in the wealthy part of town, there were broad sidewalks on both sides of the road, in addition to a grassy median strip between the lanes of traffic.

"I hope you know what you're doing," O'Rourke said. But he followed the directions.

The officer opened the front door of O'Rourke's car and leaned in. Then he opened the back door on the driver's side and leaned in again. He took a deep sniff and his nose wrinkled. He stood up, outside the car, and pressed the button on his shoulder-mounted mic.

"Uh, this is Car 23-99. I'm on Blackstone at President," he said. "I have a possible 10-55. Be advised of a VIP situation."

"Roger 23-99," the dispatcher responded. "10-55 at Blackstone and President. Request Command Officer. Repeat, request Command Officer."

"What the hell is going on?" Freddie O'Rourke called from the sidewalk. "Can we speed this up? I gotta pee."

I WAS SITTING in the front seat of a plainclothes sedan driven by Lt. Dave Andrade. We were about a block away on the southbound side of Blackstone, watching the whole thing and listening to the radio calls.

"You sure you got him, Jules?" Dave asked me.

I held up an empty pint bottle of Philadelphia blended whiskey. "I emptied the whole bottle of this cheap rot gut in his back seat foot well," I said. "His car smells like a whiskey refinery."

Andrade, watching the street, held up his hand. "Wait," he said, "Here comes the cavalry."

We watched as a TV news truck from one of the local stations parked behind Freddie O'Rourke's car. The rear door of the truck flew open and a cameraman, his TV camera on his shoulder, jumped out and began filming.

"My, my," I said. "What bad luck Freddie's having today. First he gets pulled over for DUI and then there's a TV news camera there to record the whole thing."

Andrade chuckled. "Yeah, I wonder how that happened. You would think somebody tipped them off. Not that those guys don't monitor the police frequency all the time."

In short order, two more Providence squad cars pulled in, blue lights flashing and before long the place was crawling with officers. People walking up and down Blackstone stopped to watch. I could see Freddie O'Rourke in the midst of all this, his hands waving as he tried to figure out what had happened and try to deny he had been drinking. Of course, he *had* been drinking, with his usual lunchtime martini. But the police smelled the whiskey I had dumped in his car, and they naturally assumed the worst. He would be asked to blow into a breathalyzer and perform a field sobriety test and he would likely be hauled downtown and booked. At least, that's what I was hoping for.

Andrade started up his car and we glided slowly down Blackstone, watching the scene across the median strip. Then he speeded up and headed back to the public safety headquarters on Washington Street, on a bluff above I-95 behind the Civic Center. I had met him there earlier.

"I'm guessing the Judge is gonna have some 'splainin' to do," Andrade said. "Hope he gets a judge that listens better to him than he ever did to anyone else."

"Fred O'Rourke has been an asshole for three decades," I said. "He deserves everything he gets."

"But you're not bitter, right Chief?" Dave said to me, with a smile.

"Me?" I said. "Nah. I'm only interested in justice for all."

"Yeah," Dave said, "That's what I remember learning from you in Little Penwick, way back when. Everybody gets justice."

"Sooner or later," I said, looking out my window at the city passing by. "Sooner or later."

CHAPTER
6

I WAS BACK home later that afternoon, sitting at my dining table and sifting through more of the files. I heard a car crunch up my driveway and a minute later, Siggi came in the back door from the deck.

"Yum," she said, sniffing the air. "What are you making?"

"I found a package of venison in the freezer," I said. "So I decided to make a nice stew for tonight."

"It's supposed to snow," she said, taking off her overcoat and hanging it up on the pegs by the door. "It smells like snow out there."

"Well, I'm not sure what impending snow smells like, but since the weather idiot said it's supposed to start coming down around seven, I will accept that you can smell it coming."

"You can't smell it?" she asked.

"Not with all that briny ocean out there, I can't."

She came over and gave me a kiss and a hug.

"Whatcha reading?"

I waved a hand across the table. "These are all the files on the Donna Dixon case," I said. "So far, I haven't seen anything unusual or out of the ordinary. But I've just gotten started."

"Give it time," she said. "If there's something there, you'll find it."

I began restacking papers, trying to free up at least enough space for the two of us to eat at the table. Siggi went into the kitchen, looked inside the slow cooker that was bubbling away with venison, carrots, potatoes and celery in a rich brown sauce. That was my secret: the sauce was made by my emptying a bottle of Guinness Stout into the pot. She gave it a stir, just for general purposes, and then made us a cocktail: a generous splash of bourbon on the rocks with a dollop of water. She peeled two thin curly slices of rind off a lemon and dropped one into each glass. She poured some peanuts into a shallow dish and brought it all back to the table and sat down next to me.

"Skál" she said, and we clinked glasses.

Siggi turned on the television and tuned in one of the local stations that had news before the six o'clock dinner hour. The anchors were talking about the Superior Court judge in Providence stopped earlier that afternoon for alleged drunk driving. They went to a live report from one of their newsbabes at the scene.

"Judge Frederick O'Rourke, a senior judge in the Superior Court, was stopped today near his home on the east side of Providence on suspicions of driving under the influence," she said, looking into the camera. "O'Rourke was tested with a breathalyzer and then taken to the Public Safety Complex for further processing. Police have not released results of the test as yet. Back to you, Jennifer."

Siggi turned the television off.

"Did you do that?" she asked me? Her voice was quiet. But I could tell she was worried.

"Do what?" I asked. "I didn't arrest the man. Nor was I the one driving around drunk. I've been here working my case and making dinner."

She looked at me like she didn't believe me. But she didn't say anything further. At least, not until an hour later when we were enjoying the venison stew along with a French baguette and a glass of a nice California cabernet. It was, if I do say so myself, quite excellent and I was enjoying the hell out of it.

Which is when I noticed Siggi was looking at me. With her look that said she had something to talk about. Which is different from her usual *I adore you and everything about you* looks. Which are, now that I think about it, vanishingly rare.

"What?" I said, playing the role of the dumb straight man.

She toyed with her wine glass for a moment.

"You never talk about it," she said finally. "We've never really talked about it. That can't be healthy."

"Talk about what?" I asked, I thought logically.

"You see?" she said. "You're evading the question. It's like you want to pretend it never happened. That's not good, Julius. It did happen. You need to talk about it or it will eat you alive."

This time I paused. And finished the inch of wine left in my glass and then filled it up again. I was going to need the wine reinforcement.

"If we are talking about what I think we're talking about, I don't like to talk about it because it was not a pleasant experience in my life," I said. "It happened. It's over. I lived through it. I'd like to forget all about it."

She sighed. "*That's* the part that's not so healthy," she said. "You've got to talk about it. Even if it's unpleasant. You're bottling up all the anger. All the resentment. Which is very Taurus of you, to be the strong silent type. But you need to let those bad memories and experiences out. Drag them into the light and look at them again. Yell and scream if that's what you have to do. I can handle it. But you can't just keep all those feelings bottled up inside forever. It will kill you."

I nodded like I was thinking about it. But my stomach began to hurt and it wasn't from my cooking. I hated these domestic scenes. On the other hand, what she was saying was probably correct. Which made it harder.

"Look," I said, "I got royally screwed, OK? Preston Knox did a nice little number on me to protect the trafficking operation that blondie chick was running. I shoulda seen that coming but I didn't. Maybe twenty-six years as chief made me too comfortable, thinking I was untouchable. That part is on me."

I sipped some more wine. It helped.

"So I let my guard down and Knox had me sent to jail," I continued. "That part of the story sucks, big time. Jail is no fun, ever. But I managed to survive. You suck it up and do what you have to do to survive."

"What did you have to do?" Siggi asked. "Please tell me."

I thought for a moment or two. "It wasn't as bad as it might have been," I said. "If I had really done something wrong and they threw me in the ACI for a long sentence, it probably would have been different. Cops in jail don't usually last very long in the general pop. But in my case, everyone knew that it was a set up, all political bullshit. The guards knew my being there was bullshit and that I would be out sooner rather than later. So they still considered me as one of the family and they looked out for me. So I was kind of the jailhouse celebrity, someone it might be good to get close to, maybe I could help them out once I got out. Much better than being that bastard who sent someone up the river and who now has to worry about being shivved every time you take a shower."

"So you weren't in danger?" she asked.

I shook my head. "I wouldn't say that," I said. "No matter what, you have to protect yourself. It's the first rule of jail: protect yourself."

"How do you do that?"

I shrugged. "You got to be constantly aware," I said. "Everywhere, all the time. Most of the time you can see them coming. Some hothead with nothing to lose decides he's gonna get revenge for whatever he thinks they did wrong on him by taking it out on me. In the yard. In the cafeteria. In the cell block common room. You see it coming. Or someone tells you its coming. Either way. You take steps."

"Steps?"

I smiled. Grimly. "You really don't want to know," I said. "It's not a nice place, jail. Filled with people who aren't exactly church-goers. And they all think they're bad asses. So sometimes, you just have to be a bigger and badder bad ass than they are. Or think they are."

"You had fights?" she asked. She looked worried.

I laughed. "Not exactly," I said. "Not like in a ring, with a referee and ten rounds under the lights. More like a head banging to get their attention and then a little lecture. I was lucky. Didn't have too many of those, and, like I said, the guards were mostly on my side, mostly looking out for me."

Siggi got up, came over and put her arms around me, hugging me tightly.

"I was so worried," she said. "I didn't sleep for the first month you were gone."

I hugged her back. "I know," I said. "I'm so sorry you had to go through all that. But it's over now. In the past. I'm here. I'm back. I'm safe. Life goes on."

Her arms tightened even more. But she said nothing. For a while.

"Are you sure you didn't have anything to do with the judge getting arrested today?" she said, her voice muffled against my neck.

"He was arrested by the Providence police," I said. "Not by me."

I didn't like hiding anything from Siggi. She didn't deserve that. But this was my fight, not hers. And it was my desire to get revenge. In part because of what she had to go through while I was gone. She might not want revenge. But I wanted it for her. And for me. And we were going to get it, one way or another.

CHAPTER 7

The next morning, Siggi left after breakfast and I got back to my case files.

The Little Penwick PD had followed the conventions when they started interviewing witnesses in the case. They had started with the parents, Harold and Betty Dixon. They interviewed them together and then separately, standard procedure as any discrepancies in the stories would likely come out the more times they had to tell their stories. But in this case, the stories of the parents hadn't changed.

They had moved on to interview the four surviving siblings of Donna Dixon. The two youngest kids were interviewed in the presence of a state-provided guidance counselor due to their tender ages. The two older Dixon children each sat for two interviews by two different police personnel. Again, this was deliberate to make sure their stories held up over multiple tellings. Again, their stories did not change.

The police also called in Donna's boyfriend, Charlie Stine. But his alibi—that he had spent all of the day Donna disappeared with a group of friends at the beach—held up. Several boys testified that Charlie had been at the beach all day. A teenager employed by the town of Little Penwick as a lifeguard at the beach swore he had seen Charlie at the beach with his friends. Some adults who spent time at the beach that day remembered seeing the boys and Charlie. He was ruled out as a suspect early on. The police spoke to several other classmates and friends of Donna Dixon, but no new information came forth.

I read the transcripts of the interviews with Harold Dixon carefully. As always, the first suspects are those closest to the victims. But Harold insisted that his relationship with his middle daughter was fine; there were no issues between the two, he claimed. His wife and the other children backed that assertion up. Harold did admit that his wife had spoken to Donna earlier in the summer about her relationship with the Stine boy: she had expressed concerns that she was getting "too serious" with the boy. Harold said—and Betty concurred— that they had been concerned that Donna might be embarking on a sexual relationship with Charlie, if she hadn't already, and her mother just wanted to express her concerns to her daughter about that and the possible ramifications to the girl's health and future.

Catherine Dixon, the oldest sibling, told her interviewer that she and Donna had had some conversations about these parental concerns. They had laughed a bit over the subject, she said, and said that Donna had assured her that while she 'liked' Charlie, she did not consider him to be a serious boyfriend. He was someone she liked to hang out with, someone she could show to her friends as her 'boyfriend' for social purposes, but certainly not someone she was planning to settle down with. Catherine's statement said she wasn't totally sure if Donna was having sexual relations with the boy. He told police they had made out a few times, but nothing further. I thought about the medical examiner's report that said Donna was not a virgin. So she had sexual relations with someone. But who? If not Charlie, who? It was an unanswered question.

I picked up the next piece of paper in the stack. It was the crime report filed by Roger Hart, the patrol officer who found the body. That file was check-the-boxes cut and dried, but there was a followup interview that happened several days after the murder. Conducted by an investigator from the state crime lab, it just led Hart through the timeline of the two days in question and he explained where he had been and what he had done.

I picked up the phone and called Buzzy Franklin, the Little Penwick PD's chief of detectives. Actually, he was the only detective on the force. But Buzz knew everyone in town and was also connected to lots of law enforcement people all around the state. He kept his finger on the pulse of what was happening in nearby towns and cities.

"Chief," Buzz said when he came on the line. "How you likin' retirement?"

"Soon as I retire, I'll let you know," I said. "Question: we used to have a patrolman on the force, thirty years ago now, name of Roger Hart. You got any idea where he is today?"

Buzz laughed. "Roger the Dodger," he said. "Yeah, last I heard he was living up in Fall River with his mother. Should be retired by now. He's almost as old as you are."

"Kiss my ass," I said gruffly. "Why'd you call him Roger the Dodger?"

"He was a little before my time," Franklin said. "Come to think of it, so were you. But the scuttlebutt was that Hart was always a good one for getting out of a bad shift. Like overnight in a blizzard or traffic duty at the beach on the Fourth. He'd always ask to swap shifts with someone else during those times. Hence, the Dodger. Hey … wasn't he on the force when you were just starting out?"

"He was," I said. "But I barely remember him. I was a newbie, and he left the department not too long after I started. Our paths just didn't cross that often."

"Why are you asking about him?" Franklin wanted to know.

"I'm taking another look at the Dixon case," I said. "Hart was the officer who found the body. I thought I might go talk to him."

"The Dixon case?" Buzz whistled softly. "That one was strange from the get-go. Nobody saw nothing. Nobody said anything. Nobody had any evidence. All we had was one dead girl."

"You remember that one?"

"Me? Naw," he said. "I came on years after that case. But I keep a list of all the cold cases in my desk drawer and once a year or so I take it out and look at it again. See if anything jumps out or has changed. That case started with a blank slate and hasn't changed in … how many years has it been?"

"Thirty," I said.

He whistled. "Well, good luck to you and the Red Sox.

Hang on a sec." I could hear the sound of computer keys clicking on his desk. "Here it is. This is the last known address for Roger Hart." He read me the information. I jotted it down in my notebook.

"Thanks," I said. "Let's do lunch one of these days."

"Sure thing, chief," he said. "I can be easily purchased with a cheeseburger and fries."

I hesitated. "Hey, while I got you, have you spoken with Roger Worrell lately?"

"Been a couple of months now," he said. "He's in one of those assisted living joints over in Middletown. They tell me he's got the dementia. Kinda sad. He's not totally lost in la-la land, but he's on that road and heading down it slow but sure."

"That sucks," I said. "I was going to chat with him, too. See if he remembers anything about this case that might have been hinky."

"Wouldn't expect too much," Buzz said. "Maybe if you catch him on a good day."

"Right," I said. "Thanks for all the info."

We rang off.

CHAPTER 8

A COUPLE OF days later, I drove up to Fall River to meet with Roger Hart. I had called him, told him what I was doing and arranged for a time to come speak with him. He had sounded interested in revisiting the Dixon case and said he wanted to be helpful.

"That's an old case," he said said to me. "But I think about her every now and then. Always wondered what had happened to her."

Hart lived on the east side of the old mill town, not far from Watuppa Pond, one of the city's main water reservoirs. I found his street a block off Wilson Road. There were maybe ten houses on the street, all looking like they had when built in the 1950s—one story houses with white clapboards and black shutters, a concrete stoop outside the front door with a sidewalk running down to the street. Driveway to one side, leading to a one-car garage and a small square of lawn in the front, on either side of the sidewalk. I knew these houses had three small bedrooms, one bath, a dining room, living room and kitchen. Some had basements but others were built on a concrete slab. They all dated from the post-World War II era and were designed to be small, solid and affordable for the returning vets.

Hart's house was down toward the end of the street, his lot backing onto a wooded area. The lawn was neatly tended and surrounded by a three-foot chain link fence, which didn't look high enough to keep anything either in or out. Deer, dogs and marauding kids could leap it in a single bound.

I parked on the street in front and walked up the sidewalk to the stoop, climbed the three steps and knocked on the door. After a brief wait, the door opened and Roger Hart peered out at me. He was now an old man, probably in his late seventies. His hair was now white and his face wrinkled and jowly. He stood around six feet and seemed fairly fit. He was wearing brown chinos and a flannel shirt and had a pair of thick-rimmed glasses folded and stuck in the pocket of his shirt.

"Come, in, come in," he said, waving me into the house. The front door opened into the living room, which contained a Victorian-style sofa with carved wooden legs and a sculptured upholstered back. A big matching wingback chair sat off to one side. Both sofa and chair were covered in thick see-through plastic, a style I remembered from the Sixties. Two wooden end tables framed the sofa and each one held a green and gold Quoizel lamp with a little brass-and-ball pull chain dangling down. Opposite the sofa, underneath the front windows, sat a flat-screen television on a low wooden table. There was a polished Windsor chair off to one side. An old landscape print of a mountain scene hung on the wall behind the sofa and there was a three-shelf knickknack cabinet hanging on another wall. It was full of glass figurines, cups and saucers, some framed photographs of old people and other things. I noted that the knickknacks and the shelfs they sat on were dust free and polished. There was a cocktail table in front of the sofa that was covered on top with two round lace doilies that once upon a time might have been white, but had now faded and aged into beige.

"Nice place," I said, sitting down as directed at one end of the sofa. It squeaked when I sat on the plastic seat cover. "You lived here long?"

"About fifteen years," Hart said, standing. "I moved back here to take care of my mother when she had her first stroke. Took care of her until she died and then just decided to stay. It's a solid house, doesn't take too much to keep it up and I like the neighborhood."

He motioned towards the back of the house, where the kitchen was. "You want some coffee?" he asked. "I can make some up pretty quick."

I nodded and smiled at him. "That would be great, thanks," I said.

He disappeared into the back of the house. I took the time to look around. The carpet looked recently vacuumed, which matched with the well dusted knickknack shelves and the polished tables. Roger Hart might be an old retired guy living alone, but he obviously took pride in his house and took care of it. I wondered if he had been trained, or browbeaten, into these habits by his late mother. The house was certainly neat and clean and the yard outside was neatly mowed and well tended, but there wasn't much about the place that spoke to Hart's own personality.

"Here we are," Hart said, coming back into the living room with a tray containing two mugs steaming with coffee, a small white ceramic pitcher of milk and a sugar bowl. He put the tray down on the cocktail table.

"Mother wouldn't permit any food or drink in the living room," he said, handing one of the mugs to me. "But I always said rules are made to be broken."

I smiled and took a tentative sip of the coffee. It was instant. I tried to keep my face neutral. I had sworn to myself that once I was out of jail, where they also served truly awful instant coffee, I would never drink the stuff again. But, to be polite, I did.

"So you're looking at the Dixon case again," Hart said. He sat down on the other end of the sofa and poured some cream and sugar into his mug. "You must have drawn the short stick on that assignment."

I chuckled and nodded in agreement. "Yeah, there isn't much to go on," I said. "That's why I wanted to stop by and see what you can remember. I'm hoping that maybe some new memory comes out after all these years."

He nodded and sipped at his coffee. "I get it," he said. "Well, the first I heard that the girl had gone missing was the morning after. At roll call, they told us Donna hadn't reported to work the day before and nobody could find her and the family was worried. We were told to keep an eye out during patrols that morning."

"Did you know the girl?" I asked. "Had you ever met her or come across her before?"

"No," Hart said. "I don't think so. If I had, I don't remember. I mean, I did all the things anyone in the department would do. You know, do a talk at the school or stop and talk to kids at the playground or on the athletic fields. But I don't believe I had ever met Donna Dixon before."

"How about the rest of her family?"

He shook his head. "I knew the Dad, Harold," he said. "He had come into the station, maybe a year before his girl went missing. He wanted to talk about something. I don't really remember what it was, but it was something like complaining about a neighbor's dog barking late into the night or something like that. Just a typical citizen complaint. I told him we'd send someone out to the neighborhood to listen and see if any ordinances were being broken. We chatted a little. I found out he was a teacher over at Portsmouth High. But that's about it. I don't think I ever met the mother of the girl, or the other kids. Might have, but I just can't recall."

"So tell me what you did that morning, after roll-call, when they told you to watch out for Donna Dixon."

He sipped some more coffee while he thought. He appeared to enjoy it.

"I think I mostly did the usual," he said. "We all had our routes. It was June, so I made sure to make run over to The Heights. Chief wanted us to show a presence so the rich folk…" He stopped and laughed a little. "Well, hell, you became chief a few years later," he said. "You know all about the summer crowd at The Heights and showing the flag and all that."

"Yeah," I said, "I do." Hart was right. Little Penwick, with its extensive oceanfront real estate, is a summer haven for the wealthy elite who owned summer homes, both in the exclusive Heights neighborhood and elsewhere along the coast and river front. The population of the town doubles and triples between Memorial Day and Labor Day when the second home-owners come down from Manhattan and Boston and Providence and Hartford to air out their huge Gilded Age mansions, the Deco cottages, the old farmhouses on their forty acres and the rambling ranch houses. Most had magnificent views of the ocean, while others are wrapped in the ancient farm fields or tucked away in the swampy woods.

Little Penwick made a fortune from the property taxes on these generational estates, especially since the town didn't have to provide a lot of services in return. The second-home crowd didn't send their children to be educated in Little Penwick schools, didn't need year-round police or fire services and if the town plows were a little late in getting around to clear the fancy streets on which they lived, well, the owners usually weren't even there to complain.

But as chief of police, I always made sure to send regular patrols during the summer months down those wealthy streets, making a show of force to the seasonal homeowners. And I made an effort to get to know as many of these part-time citizens as I could, showing up where they played in Little Penwick: the yacht club, the golf club, the garden club and the beach club. If the homeowners knew we were patrolling their streets, and if they had a personal connection with me or someone else on the force, they would pay their hefty property tax bills every year without complaint.

"Anyway," Hart continued, "I made my usual rounds, but kept an eye open. I remember I drove down to the playground by the elementary school that morning, just for a look-see. But there was no one there at all."

"Then you went by the Kennedy Farm," I said.

"Yeah," he nodded. "I think it was late morning, around eleven, I drove up Main Road, turned into the parking lot at the farm stand. I think there was another patrol car in the lot. Probably the chief of detectives or someone to talk to the proprietors. I turned around and headed back south on Main."

He paused, remembering that day from thirty years ago,

"You know the set up there," he said. "The farm stand and parking lot sit in the middle of the apple orchard. The peach trees are further out back. And just south of the orchard is another plot, probably three or four acres, surrounded by a stone wall. It was planted in corn, with the orchard behind. They had planted early that year and the corn was doing pretty good. You know the old saying 'knee high by the Fourth of July,' right?"

I nodded.

"Well, it was about ten days before the Fourth but the corn was at least knee high," he said. "Maybe higher. Anyway, I drove south on Main coming out of the lot and continued on past that field of corn. That's where I saw the glint."

He paused again and I watched him thinking back.

"I almost kept going," he said. "It was just a quick glimpse, that flash. Something shiny caught my eye. Could have been anything …a soda can or a piece of tin foil or anything, really.

But maybe because we were looking for something, maybe that's why I decided to stop and take a closer look."

"It was good police work," I said. "You were alert, looking for anything out of the ordinary. Like you said, it would have been easy to ignore, to overlook. But you didn't."

Hart sighed. "Yeah, I guess," he said. "Though I wish it hadn't been me that found her. That was pretty tough."

"Go on," I said.

He shrugged. "So I parked the car, climbed over the wall and walked down through the corn to the side of the orchard. I saw the bike first. It was lying on its side in the grass, next to an old apple tree. When I got up to it, I looked back down the row of corn and there she was."

"Did you see anything else at the scene?" I asked. "Footprints? Anything left behind?"

He shook his head. "Nope," he said. "I backed away, went back to the car and called it in. It wasn't five minutes before that cornfield was jumping with folks. Pretty big deal for Little Penwick, y'know? I helped them put up the crime scene tape and then stood back and watched while all the lab boys from the state came in and did their thing. Man, they musta taken a thousand photos, every which way. Hour or two later, I was told to keep the media guys away. There were TV trucks from all three stations in Providence and one from up in Boston. It was crazy."

"When did you write up your statement?"

"That night," he said. "It was after dinner. We were still at the scene out there until then. But Chief Worrell told me to write down what I saw and what I did and to do it before

I went home. While it was still fresh, he told me. So I did. I think it was close to midnight before I got home. Never got overtime for that day, either."

He smiled at me crookedly and I remembered his nickname: Roger the Dodger.

But I nodded back at him. I was just a junior patrolman that day, but even I could recall working through the day and into the night. A murder was a big deal for Little Penwick, and we had all considered it an all hands on deck kind of event.

"You left the department not long after that incident," I said.

"I did," Hart said.

"You wanna tell me why?"

He shrugged. "I had been thinking about leaving the force," he said. "Been thinking about it for some time. Maybe a year. I talked with Chief Worrell about it. Part of it was the money, which wasn't that great. But I was ready to do something else, I think. I thought after the case died down a little it was the right time."

"What did you do next?" I asked.

"I worked in private security for a few years," he told me. "Some mall security, other night watchman gigs here and there. Then a few years later, I got a job with the school system here in Fall River."

"Doing what?"

"School resource officer," he said. "Few years at one of the elementary schools and then at the middle school. Worked there more than ten years, then I retired for good."

"Did you like working at the schools?"

"Yeah, mostly," he said. "Kids are kids. Most of them are great. Few of them are monsters. Sort of like adults."

"That's for sure," I said. I glanced around the room and noticed there was nothing that indicated Roger Hart had ever worked in the public schools. No pictures of him with kids, no ribbons or plaques. Maybe they're in his bedroom, I thought.

"Anything else you remember?" I asked.

Hart shook his head. "Don't think so," he said. He paused. "You think we'll ever find who did it?"

"Yes," I said. "I think we will."

I stood up and shook Hart's hand, thanked him for the coffee and his time and left. As I drove away, I looked back and saw him standing in his front doorway, looking out at me.

CHAPTER 9

THE NEXT MORNING I was drinking my coffee and thinking about the Dixon case when I heard tires crunching on my driveway. I waited, heard steps on my back deck and the door opened. Gus Haddock came in.

"Junior," I said in greeting. "Coffee is fresh."

"Where's Siggi?" he asked. He went into the kitchen and poured himself a cup.

"She stayed at her place last night," I said. "I think her daughter came over for dinner."

"You weren't invited?" he asked.

I shrugged. "I'm always invited," I said. "But I was busy working. Reading the Dixon files. Comparing notes. So I begged off."

Gus shook his head. "I don't think I'll ever figure out your relationship," he said.

I laughed. "Here's a hint: we don't try to figure it out either," I said. "We just live the way we want to. It seems to work out pretty good."

"You recommend this on-again, off-again stuff for me?" he asked.

"Nope," I said. "I recommend you find a woman who loves and accepts you for what you are, and then figure out the best way to live so you're both happy. Makes life a lot simpler."

He shook his head as if to clear it of cobwebs.

"What's up, son?" I asked. I knew Junior pretty well, and I knew he wouldn't take the time to stop in to say hello if he didn't have something on his mind. He did.

"I took a call yesterday from the Attorney General," he said.

"Did you now?" I said. "And how is my good friend Preston Knox?"

"He's upset," Gus said.

"Good," I said. "What about?"

"He thinks you're stalking him," Gus said. "He wants me to tell you to stop."

I laughed. Got myself another cup of coffee. We were drinking a Kona blend I had found online. A little less expensive than 100 percent Hawaiian beans sourced from the Big Island, but close enough: it still had those golden notes at the base and a tasty mouthfeel. Plus, it was real coffee.

"He mentioned what happened to Judge Parker and Freddie O'Rourke," Gus said. "He seems to think you were behind both of those incidents. He thinks he's next."

"He got any proof it was me?" I asked. "And, by the way, he's right. He is next."

"Dad," Gus said with a sigh. "You can't slash and burn your way through the state's judicial ranks to get revenge. That's wrong on so many levels."

"Who's slashing and burning?" I said. "It looks more like a careful sniper's campaign to take out some wrong-doers. One at a time and from a safe distance. Besides, neither Maryann Parker or Freddie O'Rourke has lost their job. They just got a little bad PR for a few days. They'll live."

"So it was you," Gus said.

"Prove it," I said. "And I'll surrender."

Gus shook his head. He knew he couldn't. What's more, *I* knew he couldn't.

"You gonna do the same to Preston?" he asked. "Find something to embarrass him with?"

I shrugged. "If it was me doing all this, then he'd be next on the list," I said. "But it isn't me. So maybe poor ole Preston is crapping his drawers for no good reason."

"And maybe that's the thing you've got for him," Junior said. "Make him keep looking over his shoulder, waiting for the shoe to drop."

I shrugged again. "Maybe every public official should operate with that kind of concern for the voting public," I said. "Maybe that would make this a better-run state."

Gus stood up and took his cup to the sink. He rinsed it out.

"I give up," he said finally. "You can't argue with a stubborn mule. I'm just here to tell you that Knox is aware of what's going on. That means he's got some kind of strong defense in place. You should keep that in mind. Also, I'm here to ask you not to embarrass the department. Even though you're retired, you're still the former chief of police. And if you get caught doing something to the sitting Attorney General, it will have repercussions on my police force. So don't do that."

"Don't do what?" I said. "Do something to the AG? Or get caught doing something to the AG?"

My son looked at me like a hound dog that's been hooked up to a lead when it has the scent of the hare in its nose. Not happy. He left.

I POURED MYSELF another cup of coffee and went back to the Dixon files. I had started making a list of people I needed to talk to, and I looked that list over again. Former chief Roger Worrell was the first name on my list, followed by Harold Dixon, the father of the dead girl. Under that, I had put "sibs," to indicate I wanted to interview as many of Donna Dixon's brothers and sisters as I could. There were four of them, now probably living all over the country, involved with lives of their own. They might—or might not—want to revisit the death of their sister from thirty years ago.

I called the nursing home where Roger Worrell was now imprisoned and spoke to the general manager, a Mrs. Davis. She told me what Buzz Franklin had said: Roger Worrell was suffering from dementia, but it was early stages in the disease. He had been moved to the Memory Assist ward in the nursing home. Mrs. Davis told me that Worrell still had some days when he was cogent and aware of his surroundings. His daughter came to visit once a week, and he usually reacted well to her visits, chatting about children and relatives and events from the past. Other days, the bad ones, he sat and stared at the wall without speaking.

I set up an appointment to visit with him in a day or so

and rang off. Then I called Harold Dixon at his home. Dixon, like Worrell, was now in his 80s, but the father of the murdered girl seemed to still have most of his wits about him. I told him who I was and what I was doing, and he said he'd be glad to help in any way. We made an appointment for me to visit him for an interview later in the week. He sounded pleasant enough, though a little curt. Once a school teacher, always a school teacher, I thought.

But with those two appointments made, I felt like I was making some progress. I hadn't found any hard evidence much less hints that something had been overlooked thirty years earlier. But the process was now launched. I would meet with these two witnesses. Ask my questions. Judge their answers and their responses. Maybe something would fall out. That's why we do it, I thought.

I heard tires crunch on my driveway again, and this time the person coming in stopped at the back door and knocked, hesitantly. I went over and opened the door. Ben Almy was standing there. One of the Wednesdays at Jack's regulars. He was looking out at the Rockies.

"I never knew you had a great view like this," he said, before turning and smiling at me.

"C'mon in," I said. "Want some coffee? It's relatively fresh. Better than the crap that Junior Hastings makes."

"Thanks," Ben said, coming in, wiping his feet carefully on the sisal rug in front of the door, and looking around. "Siggi here?"

"Not at the moment," I said.

"Good," Ben said. "There's something I need to discuss.

Just between us."

"That sounds ominous," I said. "Take your coat off and sit down."

He left his coat on but came in and sat down in one of my living room chairs. He seemed on edge, fidgety, ill at ease. I was curious about what he wanted.

"So, the other day at lunch, you told us that you were going into the private investigation business," he started.

"Yes, I did," I said.

"Well, I may have something for you to investigate," he said, looking at me with his head cocked to one side, trying to gauge my reaction.

"Okay," I said. "What would that be?"

He paused. Took a deep breath. Looked around, then down at his hands.

"Spit it out, Ben," I said.

He looked at me and nodded.

"I need you to investigate my wife," he said. The words came out fast, as if he knew he needed to say them quickly or he'd never say them at all.

"Helen?" I said. I tried to keep a note of amazed disbelief out of my response, but I think I failed completely. Probably because I was both amazed and gobsmacked.

He nodded, casting his eyes quickly onto my face and then away.

"Why?"

That little question set off a bomb inside Ben Almy. He jumped to his feet, started toward the kitchen, then stopped and began to walk back towards the living room, then just gave up and began pacing back and forth. He looked like he was going to be sick to his stomach.

"I think she's having an affair," he said, his voice small and almost indistinguishable. In a half whisper, as if he couldn't believe it himself.

My first reaction was to go over and grab him by his lapels and shake him, hard, maybe adding a slap or two across the face in a 'snap outta it' moment. But I didn't. I stayed seated on my living room sofa, watching him pacing, and said nothing for a count or two.

"Do you have any proof or evidence?" I asked instead, keeping my voice level and emotion free. I think that's the proper interview technique taught in the Marlowe Academy of Detecting.

Ben waved his hands about, as if all the evidence I needed was right there in my kitchen, staring us in the face. "She's always gone," he said. "Or going out. Morning, noon and night. Never tells me where she's going or where she's been."

"Have you asked?"

He shook his head, no. But said "Yes. She said last night she had to go out for two hours at eight o'clock. I asked where she was going, and she said to a knitting group."

"Well, there you have it," I said. "She's in a knitting group...."

"No she isn't," he said hotly. "I've never seen her knitting anything, and we've been married twenty-seven years. Never knitted a sock or a sweater or a hat or anything, and we had three kids. I may not know much, but I know the knitting thing is a lie. I think she was meeting her lover."

"Okay, Ben," I said, "The important thing is to not go jumping to wild conclusions. I've known Helen Almy for years and years, and she would be on my list of least likely to have an affair. Not that it isn't possible, mind you. But, in my opinion, wildly unlikely."

"Then where is she going and what is she doing?" he threw out his hands in desperation. No matter how crazy I thought his story, I could tell that Ben Almy was deeply distressed. I was thinking fast, trying to figure out how I could walk through this minefield without one or both of us getting blown up.

"I don't know," I said calmly, "And neither do you. My first recommendation is that you go home right now and ask her what she's doing. I'm pretty sure there's an explanation and probably a good one. I can't imagine that your Helen is sleeping around on you."

"Yeah, well, it's always the quiet ones, isn't it?" he said, starting up his pacing again. "The ones you least expect are the ones out there catting around with everyone in town. It's what happens in all the movies. All the books."

"Okay, Ben, take it down a notch," I said. "This isn't a movie or a book. It's Little Penwick, Rhode Island, and we're talking about Helen Almy. The mother of your children. Hell, she works in the church office part-time, right? Volunteers at the PTA. Like I said, very far down on the list of potential foolers around."

"Are you going to take my case, or not?" Ben stopped and

looked at me, challenging. "Are you my friend, or not? Is it money? I can pay. Whatever you want."

I sighed. We had officially entered the minefield.

"Ben, I cannot believe your wife is fooling around," I said finally. "So any investigation I undertake to look into your wife's behavior is going to have that underlying skepticism, based on my own personal knowledge of her character and personality. But if you still want me …"

"I do," he said, his voice suddenly definitive and strong. "I've got to know what she's doing and with who," he said. "It's driving me crazy."

Driving? Or driven? I didn't say that out loud. But I sure thought it.

"Okay," I said. "Give me a week or two. I'll see what I can find out."

CHAPTER 10

I ASKED SIGGI to go with me to interview Roger Worrell, the former chief of the Little Penwick police department. Both Buzz Franklin and the nursing home's director had told me that Roger seemed to respond well to women, usually when his daughter came for a visit, so I hoped he would respond just as well to Siggi. He knew her. It was only a question of would he remember that he knew her.

The drive over to Middletown, on the island across from Little Penwick, took about a half hour. On the way, I mentioned to Siggi that I had landed my first case as a private eye.

"Really?" she said, looking at me with a big smile. "I told you! Who is it?"

"Ben Almy," I said.

"Your friend Ben?" she said. "From the boys club that meets for lunch?"

"Men," I said. "Men's Club. And yes, that's the one."

"What does he want you to do, look for his missing hairline?" She chuckled at her own joke.

"He thinks Helen is having an affair," I said.

"Dear God in Heaven," Siggi said, throwing her hands in the air. "I hope you told him to have a glass of schnapps and come back to the real world. Helen Almy is one of the dearest people in Little Penwick. Whatever makes Ben think she is stepping out on him?"

"She keeps leaving the house at odd times and for unknown reasons," I said.

"So that means she's having an affair with someone?" she said, shaking her head sadly. "What is the matter with you men?"

"Don't go dragging me into your blanket indictment," I said. "I told him he was nuts."

"Well, good," she said. "Though that's too bad about your first job. Something else will come up, I'm sure of it."

"No," I said, "I told him I'd see what I can do."

She turned and looked at me. Glared, really. But she was silent. Which was a reproach as bad as if she had starting throwing things at me. I turned red.

"He's convinced something is going on," I said. "He is emotionally distressed. I think he's crazy as a loon, but I told him I'd see what I could find out."

"So now you are spying on Helen Almy, one of my best friends?" She sounded aghast. "And one of your best friends, too. I don't think I understand."

"I'm not spying on anyone," I said. "I told Ben I'd find out what I could about what she's doing. That doesn't mean I'm going to set up round the clock surveillance on Helen Almy and have my zoom camera ready to snap some incriminating photos. I said I'd find out what I could, and that's what I will do. Quietly. Calmly."

She was shaking her head again.

"Even without looking at your chart, this is what retrograde Mercury looks like," she said. "I can tell this has bad news written all over it. You should have told him to take his sexual fantasies and place them carefully up there where the sun don't shine. I mean, really ..."

We were silent on the rest of the drive down East Main on Aquidneck until we got to the Greenview community campus, which occupied the gentle hillside that sloped down towards the Sakonnet River. Little Penwick was just across the water, maybe two miles by crow flight.

It was an hour before lunch when we were escorted into Worrell's small but tidy suite. The room was hot with not a breath of moving air. There was also a particular odor in the room, not bodily or medicinal, but something else. Maybe it was the smell of loneliness. Worrell had a bedroom, bath and a sitting room where he occupied an upholstered easy chair next to an end table and lamp, and from which he could stare at his television screen. At mealtimes, a nurse would come and escort him down the hall to the dining room where he would sit, in silence, with a dozen of his fellow residents, eat the soft, easy-to-digest foods and then get escorted back to his little suite of rooms. Not for the first time, the whole nursing home thing reminded me of jail.

Siggi and I walked in, greeted Roger and found places to sit. I thought that if I ever found myself assigned to such a place and manner of living, I would go ahead and eat a bullet.

But at the same time, I understood that others might find the security of this kind of environment and the regulated schedule of the day to be reassuring. Most people want to stave off the visit of the Grim Reaper as long as possible, even if that means jettisoning every last bit of their freedom and dignity. I, on the other hand, felt like living life on my own terms was more important than safety or security. Otherwise, I'd say to hell with it and move on to the next world.

Worrell was staring at his TV, which was playing the latest news from Fox. Some big-haired woman on the screen was complaining about something the President was doing, and telling us how wrong it was. On another channel, they'd be barking about how wonderful the President was and how lucky we were as a democracy to have him in the Oval Office. I tended to ignore the whole thing. Politics is like heroin: It feels good at the time, but eventually it will kill your soul dead.

Worrell looked up at us. He looked every bit his advanced age. His eyes were rheumy and clouded, his few remaining strands of white hair were greasy and astray, his clothes looked as wrinkled as the skin on the back of his neck. He tried to focus his eyes on us.

"I know who you are," the old man said, his voice still strong, despite an underlying wavering tone. "You're John Edward's kid, right?"

"You knew my Grandfather?" I said, a little surprised. I didn't remember him ever mentioning Roger Worrell.

"He was a good man," the old chief said, picking up a handkerchief from his lap and patting it against the corners of his mouth. "Tough old bird, but a good man."

"You got that right," I said.

"I knew your Dad, too," the old chief said. "Damn shame what happened to him in Korea. Too young. Much too young."

He turned to look at Siggi, who was wearing a pink sweater over her jeans today.

"This is my partner, Siggi Jorgensson," I said.

Worrell smiled. "Your mother came over from Iceland after the War, didn't she?" he said. "From Rek … Rekya … what is the name of that place?"

"Reykjavik," Siggi said, smiling. "How do you remember that?"

"Oh, I remember a lot of stuff," he said. "They tell me I'm forgetting a lot of stuff these days, too, but I don't remember that."

Siggi giggled.

"I remember when your Mom first came to town," he said. "There were some thought she was a Nazi spy. Or was it a commie?" He started to laugh, which turned into a hacking cough. He put his handkerchief to use. "Of course, after she learned a little bit of English, and then had you and your brother, they stopped all that nonsense."

He paused for a moment, and looked at us both.

"That's the thing about Little Penwick," he said. "Buncha witch burners. Everyone they don't know, anyone who's from someplace else, or who speaks a different language or looks different…they're witches and must be burned. Strange place."

I decided to change the subject. And I was pleased that the man seemed to have most of his marbles today. "Chief," I said, "I wanted to stop by and talk about an old case."

"Which one?" he asked.

"The Donna Dixon case," I said. "I just retired myself and I'm taking a look at some of the old and cold cases, see if I can find anything new to look at after all these years."

"Dixon," Worrell said, his eyes looking up at the ceiling while he stroked his chin thoughtfully. "Can't say I remember much about that one, sorry."

"She was 17," I prodded. "Left home one day on her bike to ride to work at the Kennedy Farm Stand place on Main. We found her the next morning, strangled, next to her bike."

"She was nekkid, right?" he said, perking up. "Not a stitch on her?"

"That's the one," I nodded. "Been reading the files on the case and it seems there were no leads to follow. Nobody saw anything, nobody said anything."

"Yeah, that one was cold from the get-go," he said, shaking his head sadly. "I tried, I really did. Called in the state boys. Called in the Federals. They all came down thinking these rubes from Little Penwick couldn't find their ass in the dark if you spotted them a cheek. Well, none of them so-called experts could find anything either. Assholes."

He shook his head again. "The FBI even whipped up a profile on that case," he said. "After two months, they sent me a copy. Said the killer was probably a male, probably around thirty to forty years old and had sexual issues. I mean, no shit Sherlock, right?" He looked over at Siggi. "I'm sorry, ma'am," he said to her, "I'm an old coot and I say what's on my mind and right out loud. Hope that doesn't offend you."

"I'll live," Siggi said and reached over to pat his hand.

"I take it you checked out all the sexual offenders on record at the time," I said.

"A'course," he said. "And we looked for any similar cases, girls strangled and left nude somewheres. There was nothing. Every possible lead turned to shit. My chief of detectives, Ricky somebody…can't remember his name …he practically went nuts on that case."

"Shuster," I said. Worrell cocked an eyebrow at me. "The detective back then."

"Oh, yeah," he said.

"The Fibbies tell you anything else?" I asked.

"Don't think so," he said. "That report is probably still lying around somewhere. You find it yet?"

"Not yet, sir," I said. "But I'm only halfway through the case files."

"It's in there somewhere," he said again. "They said the killer might be ex-police."

This time, I sat up straight. "Really?" I said. "Based on what?"

He shrugged. "Because there were no clues lying around," he said. "The profiler said the perp was either the luckiest criminal in the history of crime, or he knew what we'd be looking for and hid it, because he had once been a cop himself. We never found her clothing, for instance. Where'd that go? And where did he take her that afternoon and night? We never found out. And the scene where he dropped the body. Clean as a whistle. He cleaned up after himself. Most perps forget something or leave something behind. But not this one. The trail started cold and got even colder."

I noticed that Chief Worrell remembered a hell of a lot more about the case than I had expected. Maybe Siggi was a secret weapon after all. I made a mental note to look in the stacks of files later that afternoon and find the FBI profile report. I didn't remember seeing it.

"I've talked to Roger Hart, the officer who found the body," I said. "He left the department soon after the crime. Do you remember anything about him?"

"What was that name again, Sonny?" he asked.

"Hart," I said, "Roger Hart. He worked for the department for three, maybe four years."

"Oh, yeah," Worrell said, "Hart. His Daddy and I think his uncle were on the Cranston force. Years ago. I think one of them was killed in a bank robbery or something like that. Don't remember the details. But I think that's why he got out. I may have the dates all mixed up, though. I can't remember stuff as well as I used to."

"Don't worry about it, chief," I said, "I can go look it up."

"Yeah," Worrell said. "They got all these fancy computers and stuff now. Woulda made my job a whole lot easier." He shrugged. "But what are you gonna do? No sense cryin' over shit you can't do nothing about. You gotta work with what ya got."

A male nurse came into the room and told Worrell it was time to head down the hall for lunch.

"You two care to join me for lunch?" Worrell said, smiling crookedly at us. "The food is absolute dreck, the worst shit in the world. And they spike it with laxatives, so us old farts stay regular. But the coffee is generally pretty decent."

"We'll take a rain check on that, Chief," I said, standing up. Siggi followed my lead. "Maybe next time."

The nurse helped the old man stand up out of his chair and put one of those wheeled walkers in front of him and waited until he grasped the handle bars before letting him go.

"Good decision," Worrell said. "Worst food in Rhode Island. By a country mile." He stopped and looked over his shoulder at us from the doorway to the hall. "Been nice chatting with you. Come back sometime," he said, "And bring that pretty Swedish woman with you."

OUTSIDE, I CRANKED the engine in my SUV, but then sat there and let it idle. Then I turned to Siggi, sitting beside me in the front seat. I reached over and took her hand.

"I want you to understand that I never want to be sent to a place like that," I said. "Never, ever. I'd rather you shoot me in the head and dump my body in the sea. Tell me you understand and agree."

She smiled at me. "I understand," she said. "But I am not in control of the future. You are assuming that I will outlive you. I can't guarantee that. And who knows what kind of medical condition you will be in when you are that man's age. I can't guarantee that, either. But I will tell you that I understand and if I am left with making the decisions on that part of your life, well, I will do the best I can. That is all I can guarantee."

I sighed. It wasn't the answer I wanted, but I understood it was probably the best I was going to get.

"I'm serious," I said, throwing the truck into gear. "Just shoot me. Quick and easy."

CHAPTER 11

I DECIDED I could handle Harold Dixon's interview without the assistance of my Siggi, so I drove over to Orchard Heights Road a couple days later, after breakfast. The Dixon house looked pretty much the way I imaged it did thirty years ago. It was a two-story Colonial, what the real estate folks call a "five-four with a door." Five identical windows across the upper front-facing floor, the front entrance door in the center of the bottom floor with two windows on either side. This was a 1960s version of Colonial, though: Had it had been built in actual Colonial times it might have had dormers in the attic roof line and the front door might have been framed by columns and a roofed pediment. But this one was plain front. Five-four and a door.

I knew that Dixon's wife Betty, the dead girl's mother, had died seven years ago, never knowing what had happened to her middle child. But Harold had stayed on alone in the family home. He was now in his late seventies, long since retired from teaching at the Portsmouth high school.

The outside of the home, with its large lawn in front, flower beds and hedges at the foundation, was neatly kept. I wondered if Harold still did the yardwork or if he called on one of Little Penwick's many landscaping firms. Or maybe his kids, now grown-ups, stopped by on weekends to handle the yard chores for their Dad.

I parked the car on the street, walked up the sidewalk to the front door and rang the bell. The sound echoed inside the home. After a brief pause, the door swung open and Harold Dixon looked out at me.

He was pushing eighty. His clothes—a raggedy sweater, casual shirt and corduroy pants—seemed to hang on his frame. Just as his skin seemed to hang on his bones. He was unnaturally thin, so his sharp nose and even sharper chin pointed outwards like extended fingers. Dixon stuck out a liver-spotted hand and I shook it. His hand was all bones and papery skin and I was careful not to apply too much pressure.

"Come in, come in," the old man said, his voice wavery and thin. He led me down the central hall and into the den, which looked out over the back yard. I saw another swath of green lawn with a ten-foot row of vegetable patch inside a fence at the back of the lot. The bed was raised on a wooden plinth and was protected by a chicken wire enclosure. There are deer everywhere in Little Penwick and they come out of the swamps and woods to discover what delicious morsels the two-legged residents of Little Penwick have growing. Planting season hadn't started yet—the rule of hard-core Swamp Yankees is to not plant seeds until Memorial Day for fear of a late killing frost—so the vegetable bed was just dirt.

The den was wood paneled and the seating was arranged around a stone fireplace and mantel. Bookshelves covered one wall and a TV sat in the corner.

"I was glad to get your call," Dixon said to me as we sat down. "Very glad. After all this time, you get to thinking that nobody cares anymore."

"I can assure you that no one at the Little Penwick police department has stopped caring about finding whoever killed your daughter," I told him. "The case was always a difficult one. From the get-go, there was not a whole lot of evidence to build on. And there hasn't been much in the intervening years. But nobody has given up."

"Why now?" Harold asked, his watery eyes peering at me through his thick glasses.

I looked at the man and decided to tell him the truth. He deserved that, I thought.

"I'm mostly retired now, Mr. Dixon," I said. "My son has taken over as chief of the department, and I've been put out to pasture." He smiled at that. "That sounds a little harsher than I mean," I continued. "But it was time for a change in the department, time for new leadership. So in trying to find something useful I could do, I decided to take a look at some of the unsolved cases in our files. And the Dixon case is at the top of that list."

"Yes, I see," he said, nodding. "That's very good news. Have you made any progress?"

I shook my head. "Not yet," I said. "So far, I've mostly been reviewing the evidence and going over the investigative files that were compiled at the time the crime occurred. I'm trying to find any possible loose ends that might have been missed, anything that at the time was not considered important, but might be now."

Harold Dixon nodded. "How can I help?" he said.

"What can you tell me about the family dynamic as it was back in '91?" I said. "You still had a house full of kids back then. I think all but one was living at home that summer."

He stroked his chin and looked up at the ceiling. "Yes," he said, "I think Catherine was living in that apartment up in Providence that summer. She was old enough. She had graduated from college and was working at a store. She and a friend of hers were sharing a place up there."

"Were you and your wife okay with that?"

"Oh, sure," he nodded. "Like I said, she had graduated. She was never a great student, so we had no expectations that she'd continue her collegiate studies beyond her four years at URI. I think her mother was worried about her living by herself in the big city, but that's normal. Catherine did well. Worked for about five years, met a nice fellow and they got married. Two kids."

"That's nice," I said. "What about the other kids? Any trouble with them?"

He shook his head. "Not that I can remember," he said. "Johnny still had a year or two of college to go. He eventually got hired by one of the big jewelry companies up in Warwick. He was a computer expert and right about then computers became part of everyone's lives, so he was in the right place at the right time. Worked out well for him."

I nodded and smiled, encouraging him to go on.

"Billy and Franny were still in school, living at home," he said. "I think Franny was just in eighth grade in 1991. I'd have to look it up. But they both lived here at home."

"It must have been hard on them, losing their sister," I said.

He nodded. Then sighed. "Yes," he said, "It was very difficult on them both. They've both had their problems in the years since then. Billy got a little sideways with drugs for a time. Almost got kicked out of high school. Luckily, I had a little influence there." He smiled at me.

"And Franny…well, Franny was always our biggest cross to bear," he said, his face serious and his eyes suddenly sad. "Always was a bit of the wild child growing up," he continued. "After Donna was …after she left us, Franny got wilder. Ran away a couple of times. When she turned 18, she left Little Penwick. Left New England, in fact. She was out in California for a few years. We only heard from her from time to time."

"Did she ever come back?"

"Yes," Harold nodded. "When her mother got sick, Franny came home. Spent a year and a half nursing her, doing what she could to help." His voice trailed off and he stared out the window for a while, thinking, remembering a sad time.

"Is she still living in the area?" I asked.

"Franny? Yes," he said. "Or no…I mean, she lives up in Boston with her partner, Virginia." He looked at me sideways. I nodded. I understood what he was telling me. "They do come down to visit from time to time. They were here a month or so ago, for Easter."

"Who was Donna closest to, among the other kids," I asked. "Who would she have confided in, if she had a problem of some kind?"

He stroked his chin, thinking.

"Well, that's a good question," he said finally. "I don't know. I guess I'd say she was close to Billy. He was just a year and change older. And probably Franny. I'd sometimes think to myself that Donna liked mothering Franny. And Fran looked up to Donna and admired her back, I think. I'd guess that Donna would take any problems to either Billy or Franny, depending of course …"

"Was Donna close to your wife? Did they get along?"

Harold nodded decisively. "Oh, yes," he said. "My wife loved her children, all her children. They were the most important things in the world to her. Nothing she wouldn't do for them, any of them. She was a fine, fine woman. I miss her deeply, even now, what…almost eight years after I lost her."

I nodded. I also noted that Harold had not really answered the question.

"Was there anyone you thought might have committed this crime?" I asked. "Anyone the police overlooked? Anyone that might have been angry with Donna? From school, from the neighborhood, from activities around town?"

Harold was stroking his chin again. But he was shaking his head from side to side.

"Believe me, chief, I have thought about that," he said. "Over and over again. For thirty years. Who could have done something like that to my little girl?" He looked at me and I could see the anguish in his eyes. I imagined the sleepless nights. The long walks on the beach. The endless reexamination of events and acquaintances and circumstances. Over and over for three decades.

"At first, I was sure that Charlie Stine was the one," he said.

"The boyfriend," I said.

"Yes," he nodded. "But they told me that he was at the beach all day that day."

"With four of his friends. And a couple girls they knew. And was seen there during the afternoon by at least three adults," I said. "His alibi was rock-solid."

"So after him, I just couldn't think of anyone else who might have done such a thing," Harold said. "Just nobody. It's just so god-damned frustrating."

His voice shook. His head went down and he kept it there, hanging on his chest. His shoulders shook, briefly, before he looked up again. His eyes were watery. They looked at me in silent appeal.

I reached over and squeezed the old man's arm.

"We're still looking," I said. "Still on the case. If we can, if it's at all possible, we'll find him."

Harold could only nod his appreciation.

CHAPTER 12

When I got back home, I called Buzz Franklin at the police department.

"Hey, chief," he said, "Wassup?"

"I was wondering if you could run a BCI for me," I said. "Two, actually."

"What the hell," Buzz said, "I got nothing else to do."

I picked up on his unspoken sarcasm.

"You can say 'no,'" I said. "I won't be offended. I understand you have other work to do."

"No, that's OK chief," he said, sounding a little chastened. "It's just … well … Gus spoke to me a day or two ago. He told me you were doing some private stuff. Said you might be calling and just wanted me to make sure I wasn't stepping over any lines, y'know?"

"Sure, I get it," I said. "The boy is concerned I may upset some apple carts, poking around in old cases. But I'm looking into the Donna Dixon case, which is still open, if pretty cold. It would be good to resolve it. That's the only reason I'm asking. And I know the difference between illegal and legal."

"I got ya, chief," Buzz said. "Gimme the names."

"Francis Dixon, goes by Franny," I said, looking at my notes from the morning. "Age around 42. Lives up in Boston. Brookline, I think her father said. Has a partner, Virginia, last name unknown. I don't know her employment status." I flipped a page. "The other one is Dixon, William, middle initial unknown. Age 45. Lives in Newport, or did at one time. Probably has some ticks in his record. His Dad says he was into drugs and maybe some other stuff."

"Got it," Buzz said. I could hear his pen scratching as he wrote down the information. "Gimme a couple days. I'll get back to you."

"Thanks," I said. We hung up.

THAT DONE, I rooted around in my cardboard box of evidence from the Dixon investigation until I found the slender navy-blue folder emblazoned with the gold logo of the FBI. Psychological Profile it said on the front. I opened the file and began to read it.

1. Assimilation, it began. I understood that the FBI had reviewed the evidence gathered by the Little Penwick police as well as the state crime lab technicians who had combed over the crime scene, the girl's bicycle, the autopsy report and any of the other sparse pieces of evidence that had been left behind by the girl's killer. There hadn't been much of that. And I also knew that the FBI preferred to have an actual suspect to profile, instead of a cipher. Preferably one who had committed multiple crimes. Made it easier to run them through the psych filter. But they didn't have any of that with this case. I skipped over the lists in this section and went on to the next.

2. Classification. The author of the profile, whom I noted was a Ph.D., had analyzed the evidence and the crime scene and designated the perpetrator of the Dixon crime as "organized." This classification meant, the author explained, that the killer had advanced social skills and had likely used those social skills to gain control over the victim. It said the killer had likely planned the crime in advance and would carefully control the crime scene to leave as little evidence behind as possible.

Got that right, I thought

The profiler then pointed out one anomaly: "organized" killers typically engaged in sexual acts with the victim before killing them. This one had not. The profiler explained this was possibly part of the overall control mechanism of the killer. "By not conforming to the usual psychological patterns shown by most organized perpetrators, this one may be signaling his or her superiority. 'I'm better organized, more in control than other killers like me,' he seems to be saying," the report said.

So, this guy wanted to have sex with the Dixon girl, I thought. *Maybe he intended to have sex with her, but then, because he knew the Fibbies would lump him into a class with other nasty killers, decided to hold off. That must have taken a lot of discipline.*

There were a few more pages of psychological jargon that went mostly over my head and made my eyes cross. But near the end were a few conclusions.

"It is our assessment that this perpetrator is:

—a male, from 35-55 years of age

—has trouble with authority. Does not like being told what to do

—is organized in his life. Dresses neatly, maintains a well-kept home, presents a 'normal' outward personality in work and personal relationships

—utilizes friendliness and social connections to overcome any resistance from his victims; does not use brute force or violence

—there is a 70+ percent likelihood that he has killed before or will kill again

—has kept the girl's clothing as "a trophy" possibly to show or share with a current female relationship or family member

—it cannot be ruled out that this is someone with law enforcement background, possibly even a serving officer. Military police?

I put the file down and sat there thinking about this for a while. If I was looking for males who didn't like being told what to do, but were outwardly organized and normal, I was looking at roughly all males. That didn't help narrow down the suspect pool, at all. Former cop? Again, if I started looking into former cops in Rhode Island, I'd be looking at a list of several thousand candidates. I thought about Roger Hart, the cop who had found the body. But I hadn't picked up any bad vibes on Roger the Dodger. He seemed pretty white bread to me.

I kept going back to the assessment that the guy had killed before, or might have killed after Donna Dixon. I was close to one hundred percent sure that Rick Shuster or the state crime investigators had immediately checked for similar cases in the years leading up to 1991, looking for girls who had been abducted, stripped, possibly sexually abused, then murdered and abandoned without leaving any clues behind. That was standard operating procedure. If there had been any similar cases, the investigation would have moved in that direction.

But what about over the last thirty years? Had there been any similar cases in the area since then? I wondered. Even if there had been, would an astute investigator have linked that new case to the one in Little Penwick? That was harder to judge. I'd like to believe that every homicide investigator was thorough and would have checked for similar instances of this kind of crime. But I knew that most police departments were stretched thin and many, many cases fell through the cracks. Nobody's fault, really, just the reality of police work.

I knew that my best play was to call Buzz Franklin back and have him run a query on all the police databases for Rhode Island and probably for Bristol County in Massachu-setts and have him look for similar cases. But the current chief detective in Little Penwick was already leery of helping my inquiries too much—he had been warned by his chief not to get sucked in. Still, this was a murder case, even one that was thirty years old. Most cops would understand that solving the case was paramount. A girl was dead, and it didn't matter if her death had occurred three decades ago.

Donna Dixon deserved an answer. Whether someone's nose got out of joint wasn't important. Finding out who killed her was. But I decided to hold off on the request. I'd talk to some of Donna Dixon's siblings first, and see what I could find out. The information I needed wasn't going anywhere. I could have it called up whenever I needed it.

I stood up and stretched. Sitting and reading for so long made my back muscles tense up and ache. I stretched a little and then walked outside to get the mail out of the box. Among the usual host of bills, flyers from the supermarket, catalogs that Siggi liked to thumb through and assorted other pieces of junk mail was the copy of the weekly community newspaper, the *Newport County News*. It was a paper that had the best coverage of the local town council and school board meetings, along with profiles of local members of the garden club, high school sports and the church news.

I started to flip through it when I saw an article: *Attorney General to Address Newport Legal Society*. Preston Knox was coming to Newport to give a luncheon speech to the city's lawyers. The luncheon was tomorrow.

I smiled to myself. It's rare when the prey come willingly into the predator's own back yard. I knew where I was having lunch tomorrow.

CHAPTER 13

I FINESSED MY way into the Moorings Restaurant overlooking Bowen's Wharf on Newport's waterfront the next day. Somebody once told me that the somewhat out-of-place elegance of the exterior of this upscale restaurant was due to its former life as one of the original summer homes of the New York Yacht Club, which now operated out of its own massive granite towered building overlooking Brenton Cove on the southern shore of the harbor. The New York yachties had been summering in Newport since the Gilded Age, when many of the richest members built oceanfront "cottages" up on Bellevue Avenue: cottages of immense size, each trying to out-do the next in grandeur and status; situated on acres of carefully landscaped grounds and decorated inside with paneling and windows and archways and balconies and staircases literally disassembled from many of Europe's most magnificent castles and churches and shipped, piece by piece, to Newport.

I had called several attorneys I knew over in Newport, having gone up against their clients in various cases over the years, until I finally found one who had a ticket to the luncheon with the attorney general he wasn't going to use. I shamelessly begged until he agreed to give it to me, and picked it up on the way into town.

Newport outside of the summer season is really quite a nice place to visit: the old Colonial streets are still there, as is the round harbor bordered by the Civil-War-era Fort Adams at the entrance to Narragansett Bay. And without the masses of the summer crowds bringing traffic to a standstill, one can find a good parking space, dine at every restaurant without a reservation and walk down the usually tourist-crammed Thames Street without feeling claustrophobic.

I was wearing an actual businessman's suit, trying to blend in with the three-piece lawyers I waited in line with, as I edged up to the table upstairs in the Yacht Club room on the second floor to give the nice lady my ticket and be ushered into the private dining room, which held about 50 seats in round tables scattered around in front of the massive window walls that provided excellent and open views out across the harbor. Here in April, the moorings were slowly filling up again with boats, although there were still more buoys than boats today.

I found a seat at a table in the middle of the room, far enough away from the speaker's dais and table at the front so that Preston Knox wouldn't notice me. At least, not right off the bat. I was a little concerned that if he saw me there before he started speaking, he might have me tossed out like a rotten fish. But I had a back-up plan: if ejected, I planned to treat myself to a cold beer and a big bowl of clam chowder at the Black Pearl just around the corner on Bowen's Wharf.

There were already four other lawyers sitting at my table for eight. I nestled in between a middle-aged woman with big blond hair and a skinny guy in a blue business suit who had a dark shadow of unshaved whiskers streaked across his chin and cheeks. He looked young, to me, in his late twenties, maybe. I guess that unshaven look is OK with lawyers of a certain age. To me, it made him look like a criminal, which, to my way of thinking, is never a good look for lawyers.

There was a cash bar at the back of the dining room, but I ignored it. I sipped my glass of cold water and nibbled on some crackers that had been placed in a basket on every table. I suspected that chowder of some kind was on the lunch menu. I chatted briefly with the big-haired lady on my right. When she found out I was the former chief of police for Little Penwick, she looked at me questioningly. But she didn't make me explain how I had obtained a ticket to the Newport Bar Association event. Which I could have done, if forced to.

Over the next half hour, the noise in the room steadily grew as more members of Newport's honored bar filed in, bought a drink, and stood around chatting with each other. Finally, the woman who had been taking tickets at the front came in, walked up to the dais in front and, speaking into the microphone, told everyone to find a seat and sit down in it, the luncheon was about to be served.

Preston Knox still hadn't made his appearance. I relaxed and enjoyed the food that a small squadron of servers brought out to our tables: clam chowder to start, and a choice between a grilled cod filet or a barbecued chicken entree of some kind.

I went for the chowder and fish, since The Moorings is a well respected seafood house in Newport, and it was excellent.

We had all been eating for about twenty minutes when Knox finally strolled in, flanked by a large black man wearing a navy blue windbreaker jacket, playing the role of the attorney general's security guy. I didn't remember Knox ever having a full-time security guy before—he usually just had a uniformed statie on hand when he needed some beef. Rhode Island's state police dress for success: they wear wide-brimmed round Stetson hats, run leather straps across their chests and around their waists and sport highly polished riding boots that run up and over their calves. I always wondered what they'd do if suddenly caught in a gunfight while dressed like one of Mussolini's palace guards and decided that most of them would duck and run. To avoid scuffing their boots or something.

Knox, wearing his usual snappy suit, his slightly greying hair gelled back, glad-handed his way through the room until he finally reached the table in front, where he sat down and began chatting with the tickets woman, who was apparently in charge of this meeting of the great legal minds of the City by the Sea. I finished my cod and nodded at the server who was starting to make the rounds with a coffee pot. Other servers began clearing the plates and began bringing out a dessert, which was some kind of fruity tart thing with a meringue topping.

The woman got up, made some introductory remarks that were heavy on lawyer humor, which went over my head, and then introduced the Rhode Island attorney general.

Knox took over the microphone to enthusiastic applause with a broad smile and began talking about his love for the city of Newport and recounted some of the legal battles he had over the years in the courts over on Washington Square. I sipped my coffee to keep from falling asleep.

He went on to claim that both he and his audience were engaged in the same honorable profession: the search for justice. "Of course," he said, "As the Attorney General, elected by the people, my role is slightly different than yours." It was a not-so-subtle reminder that he, Knox, held power, while the rest of the room, just a bunch of $500-an-hour ambulance chasers, were perhaps a few degrees above pond scum. But having insulted them all to their faces, he went on to reel off a few more platitudes and word cabbages, quoted John Marshall, held up a worn copy of the U.S. Constitution taken from the pocket of his suit coat, and even told us of the promise he made to his mother on her deathbed to "serve all the people."

I was glad at this point that I had not delved into the dessert, for I feared I would be hurling chunks of it across the table at what I was hearing. In the last part of his speech, he began reeling off a list of "reforms" he said were necessary to ensure that elusive goal of "justice for all." We all understood that he was now talking about his upcoming gubernatorial campaign. I looked around and saw the other attendees listening, nodding in places, looking at each other now and then with little smiles and winks. I couldn't quite discern what most in the room felt about Knox's speech, but it felt like many of them were eating it up. I guess fancy lawyers don't get out that much.

He finally brought his speech to a merciful end, and everyone applauded. One or two stood up to clap, no doubt hoping to get an appointment to the campaign committee or maybe even a job in the future Knox administration. I didn't applaud. The big-hair blond next to me noticed.

"You didn't like his speech?" she whispered to me.

I shrugged. "I don't do politics," I said.

"Oh, that's right … you're a cop," she said. "Must be a Republican."

I just smiled at her.

The woman running the event got on the microphone again. "General Knox says he would be happy to field a few questions," she said. "Please stand up if you'd like to be recognized."

The first few questions were about legal issues. He was asked what he could do to speed up the appeals process. He was asked about some legislation working its way through the state legislature that change the way insurance companies would handle unfair claims suits. He spent almost ten minutes talking about that one. Apparently a great many members of the Rhode Island Bar are involved with suits against or involving insurance companies.

I stood up. The ticket woman pointed at me.

"Yes, General Knox," I said, "You are famous for having appointed a staff of all women in the Attorney General's office. Can you comment on reports that there have been several complaints about sexual harassment inside your office?"

I sat down. A buzz rose in the room as people *oohed* and *aahed*, looking around to see who had asked such a question.

Knox himself shaded his eyes with one hand as he peered out into the bright lights that illuminated the speaker's dais.

"Who asked that?" he said, talking to the woman at his side. I saw her shake her head as she told him she didn't know.

"Yes," he said finally into the mic. "I don't know where you heard that, but I can assure you it is completely inaccurate. I am proud of my record on women's issues. I am proud to have a staff of some of the finest female lawyers in New England. I am not aware of a single instance of a claim of any kind of illegal or immoral behavior in my office." His face had turned a little red, and he now looked out at the room with a big grin. "That question must have been asked by someone working for my opponent in next year's race!" he said. "Welcome to Rhode Island politics."

There was a smattering of laughter in the room. The big hair blond turned and looked at me. "Who do you work for?" she demanded. "That was a really low blow."

"So this 'believe all women' thing doesn't apply to politicians you like?" I said. "Whatever happened to you feminists? I thought you had principles."

Her mouth opened, but nothing came out. I smiled at her again, dabbed at my mouth with my napkin which I threw on the table as I stood up.

"Nice lunching with you," I said and, nodding to everyone else at my table, I made for the exit.

I got as far as the hallway outside the meeting room when there was a tap on my shoulder. I turned around to face the big black dude with the windbreaker.

"General'll like to talk to you, sir," he said, "If you don't mind."

"Not at all," I said. "I'll wait for him down in the parking lot while he campaigns."

I was perched on the fender of my SUV, arms crossed, enjoying the warm April sun on my face. I saw the security dude come out of the restaurant followed by Knox. The dude looked around, saw me, and pointed. Knox came striding over, his security man trailing by a step or three.

He stopped when he was about twenty feet away.

"Oh, Christ," he said, "Julius Haddock. I should have known."

"Hiya, Preston," I said. "How's it hanging?"

"This is it?" he said, throwing his hands out wide. "This is what you had cooked up for me? Tossing out a false accusation in front of a group of my peers?"

"They're not your peers," I said, "You're an elected official. We are working people."

Knox looked around. "Where is the press?" he said. "That's how this works, right? You accuse me of something, the press picks it up and we're off to the races. Where's the TV truck? The reporter? The camera? C'mon, I'm ready…bring them on."

"Don't know what you're talking about," I said, trying to look as innocent as I felt. "There's no press here, far as I know. I was just asking a question of my elected official. I think there's something in the Constitution about that. Maybe you could get your copy out and look it up."

Knox was still surveilling the parking lot, looking for a horde of crazed reporters. He finally realized there were none. So he looked at me again.

"What's your game, Haddock?" he said. "What do you want from me?"

I laughed. "You really just asked me that question?" I said. "You upend my life, take away my job, put me in jail for eight months and you want to know what I want? Geez, you're as stupid as you are corrupt."

"Okay, okay," he said, holding up his hands as if to ward off something. "I don't have time to stand around talking with a crazy man." He stared at me and tried to look stern. Like an Attorney General might do. "You stay the hell away from me, Haddock," he said. He looked at his security guy. "John, please take a good look at this guy. If he ever comes within twenty feet of me again, please shoot him."

"Yessir," John said, smiling.

Knox turned on his heel and strode back into The Mooring. I guess he still had some hands to shake and babies to kiss. Politicking is never done. His security guy stayed next to me. I guess he was worried I was going to follow Knox inside and was trying to figure out the best place to put a couple caps in me.

"Hi, John," I said, putting out my hand. "Julius Haddock. I used to be the chief of police in Little Penwick."

He shook my hand. "Afternoon, chief," he said. "I'm not going to have any trouble with you, am I?

"Me?" I said, trying to sound amazed. "Naw. But you might have some cleaning up to do with ole Preston in there. He's pretty dirty, as I'm sure you know."

"Whatever," John said. "I got no beef with you, Chief. You got a good rep in this state with law enforcement. And you can say or do whatever you want. Just make sure you keep at least twenty feet away from him. Otherwise, I might have to do something."

"Read you loud and clear, John," I said. "I'll adapt my plan, extend it out to twenty-one feet."

He chuckled at that. "See that you do," he said. He nodded at me, turned and went back inside the restaurant.

CHAPTER 14

I ASKED SIGGI if she wanted to go on a road trip with me. I had made contact with Frannie Dixon, thanks to a phone number that Buzz Franklin had unearthed. Frannie was an orthopedic surgery nurse at Brigham and Women's hospital in Boston. Her partner Virginia, whose last name we learned was Hollister, worked as a registered nurse in the pediatrics department at Boston Children's. Since roughly half the work force in Boston is employed by one of the six or so major hospitals in the city, this was not surprising to me.

Frannie had agreed to meet me for lunch, and we had set a date and a place. That's when I asked Siggi to go with me, promising to take her to a museum, out for a nice dinner somewhere and a night in the Boston Harbor Hotel down on the waterfront. Siggi thought a little road trip would be fun.

The appointed day dawned chilly, with low scudding clouds driven across the sky by an energetic and cold north wind, keeping the warming April sunshine at bay for a while. It took us about an hour to get to the Southeast Expressway at Braintree, then another forty minutes to fight the traffic into town, through the Big Dig tunnel, out the other side and up onto Storrow Drive northwards alongside the Charles River. There were no sailboats tacking back and forth across the Charles, no Boston Pops concerts in the big shell next to the river, and no baseball team getting ready to take the field at Fenway Park on the far side of Kenmore Square. I picked up Brookline Ave., and followed it out through the marshes and weeds known as the Fens. All of the Back Bay used to be one giant smelly swamp before they filled it in, gave it romantic names and built a ballpark.

Our destination was a place called Cutty's in the heart of Brookline, a mostly residential and gentrified neighborhood north of Boston, with upscale apartment buildings, condos, streetside restaurants, cafes and bars and a few pool halls. We made it by 11:30 and even after circling through the neighborhood once or twice trying to find an empty parking space, we were able to get to the restaurant and grab a table for four in the back. Cutty's has big plate glass windows across the front, a large open counter behind which the sandwich makers do their stuff, a wall covered with the menu offerings, and a small seating area off to one side, with its Formica-topped tables and red metallic chairs.

Siggi held down the table as the lunch crowd began to build, while I went over to study the menu and order two mugs of coffee. I brought them back to the table, licking my lips.

"I take it from the drool coming off your chin that you've found something suitable to order," Siggi said, taking her coffee from me.

I made some cave-man sounds. "Meat," I said. "The most popular sandwich here is called the Roast Beef 1000. Apparently, it's been written up by every foodie magazine in the free world."

"I'm happy for you," she said. "What about us occasional vegetarians? Anything good for us?"

Two middle-aged women came up to the table, looking inquisitive.

"Are you Chief Haddock from Little Penwick?" the taller of the two asked.

I stood up and introduced myself and Siggi. The taller woman was Frannie Dixon. She had long reddish-blond hair, broad shoulders and long arms and legs. She was wearing a black cotton hoodie sweatshirt and jeans, and it looked like she had a few additional layers on underneath. The other woman, introduced to us as Virginia Hollister, was shorter and rounder, with a pleasant face, short dark hair and a metallic stud in one ear. She wore a hunter's green quilted parka and her jeans were fashionably ripped here and there. She sported a pair of thick-soled ankle-height boots that I would have called shit-kickers except that I wasn't sure if that term was still politically correct. I suspected not.

The two women sat down and we all decided what to order. I already knew, but the women examined the printed menu and discussed the options.

"I was just asking Julius what a non-roast beef fan should order," Siggi said. "Any suggestions?"

"The spuckie is real good here," Virginia said. "Roasted eggplant with olive and carrot salad."

"That sounds delicious," Siggi said. "But what's a 'spuckie?' That doesn't sound so good."

The two women laughed. "It's a Boston thing," Frannie said. "I think it's short for spucadella, which is like this Italian sandwich roll. You go down the North End and every place down there sells spuckies for lunch."

Siggi looked at me. "One eggplant spuckie for me, please," she said. "Hold the onions."

The other two chimed in—Frannie wanted the grilled cheese and Ginny the broccoli rabe with tomato jam. I went up to the counter and put in the order—including my Roast Beef 1000—and came back with drinks for the two women.

While we waited for the sandwiches to be made, we chatted. They were interested to learn Siggi was also a nurse at a local pediatrician in Little Penwick. "Frannie likes blood," Ginny said. "I'm more into kids. They dig me." As we talked, I could see that these two seemed to fit together well as a couple. They smiled at each other, touched a lot, even finished each other's sentences from time to time. They looked relaxed and happy together.

When the food came, we all dug in and the conversation died. But once the sandwiches were devoured and I got a refill on my coffee, I started in.

"As I told you on the phone," I said, "I'm taking another look at your sister's case."

"Been a long time," Frannie said, cocking her head to one side.

"It has," I agreed. "There wasn't much for investigators to go on at the time, and there hasn't been much new since.

But I'm just going back over the case, piece by piece, to see if anything new or unusual falls out."

"Okay," Frannie said. "Shoot." She giggled. "And I don't mean that literally."

Virginia laughed and gave Frannie's arm an affectionate squeeze.

"I understand that you and Donna were close as sisters," I said. "Is that how you remember it?"

"Yeah, sure," Frannie said. "I looked up to Donna. I mean, Catherine was a good sister, too, but she was almost ten years older than me. We didn't have as much in common, y'know? Donna and I liked the same bands, the same movies and stuff like that. Catherine and John were half a generation older, so they were into other stuff. So Donna, Billy and I probably had more to talk about."

"If she had a problem, would she come talk to you about it?" I asked.

Frannie shrugged. "I guess," she said. "Probably."

"Did she?"

"Not that I remember," Frannie said.

"She never came to you to talk about a boyfriend, or anyone giving her trouble?"

"Not that I recall," she said. "Of course, we talked about our parents a lot."

"What about your parents?"

Frannie sat back and blew out a long breath. Virginia reached over and held her hand in a supportive gesture.

"Well, they were pretty much a horror show," Frannie said finally.

I kept my face impassive.

"How so?"

"Well, Mommie Dearest was an alcoholic," Frannie said. "Started in on the vodka at 9 a.m. and didn't stop until she passed out, usually right after dinner. None of us could ever figure out how she managed to get through the day, especially cooking a big dinner every night, when she was blotto. But she somehow managed."

"And your father?"

"Cold, mean, lack of emotion, withheld affection, constant criticism, now and then violent," Frannie said. It was if she was describing the colors on the billboard across the street from the restaurant. Her words were spoken in a flat, emotionless, factual tone of voice.

"How awful for you," Siggi said. She had been quietly listening and watching Frannie as she spoke. Siggi knew not to interject herself into any kind of official interview, but it was obvious her reaction came straight from her heart. I felt the same way, but I had been trained to keep my own emotions out of any subject interview.

"When were you born?" Siggi asked.

Frannie smiled at her. "February 24," she said. "I'm a Pisces."

"Hmmm," Siggi said, noncommittally.

"Was your father that way with all the kids in the family?" I asked, trying to get my interview back on track.

Frannie nodded. "Pretty much," she said. "Maybe a little more with us girls,. John and Billy probably shrugged it off more than we did."

"I don't know," Virginia piped in. "I've talked to Billy quite a lot and he felt the emotional abuse. A lot. And he got hit from time to time as well."

"So your Dad could be cruel sometimes," I said. "Was he especially cruel towards Donna?"

Frannie shook her head. "Not all the time," she said. "But when you needed him for something, he always found a way to remind you that he was keeping score. 'You owe me' was one of his favorite expressions."

"You said he was occasionally violent," I said. "Did he hit you, too?"

"Yes," Frannie said. "You learned not to get into an argument with him, about anything, because he'd eventually just backhand you across the mouth. You learned to stay away, keep your head down, never engage."

"Did he hit the others? Donna?"

"She told me once that he pushed her down the stairs," Frannie said, her eyes cold with anger. "She had asked him for five bucks so she could go to the movies with her friends. He said no. She turned to walk away and he just shoved her from behind. Took a tumble down ten or twelve steps, ass over teakettle. She was lucky nothing got broke."

"How about the boys?" I asked. "He get rough with them too?"

Frannie shook her head a little. "It was different with them," she said. "He set these impossibly high standards for the boys. Like, in Little League, they had to be the stars. Had to hit home runs or be the best pitcher. If they didn't, he'd scream at them, tell them they were worthless, that they wouldn't amount to anything. Then he's make them practice in the back yard for hours and hours, until they were ready to drop." She paused and shook her head the memories. "Yeah, it was pretty much a shit show at the Dixon house."

"Did your mother try to defend you?" I asked.

"She was drunk," Frannie said. "All the time. Don't remember a day when she wasn't. And who could blame her? If I was married to a monster like that, I'd be drunk all the time, too."

"You came back home to help when she got sick," I said, remembering what her father had told me.

"Somebody had to," she said now. "God knows Father wasn't going to lift a finger. Her illness was just a sign of weakness to him. It was *her* fault. Her dying was a problem for him. The whole time I was there, I was hoping he'd get sick and die, too. But he didn't."

"What do you remember about the day Donna disappeared?" I changed the subject, hopefully to one a little less emotionally fraught.

She shrugged again. "Billy and I were just hanging around at home," she said. "Donna got ready to go to work. She was supposed to be there at noon, I think. She might have hoped that Mom could drive her over to the farm stand, but Mom was probably on her way to being comatose by then. Donna probably didn't want to get in the car with her. So she decided to ride her bike to work, which was something she did often. It wasn't that far, maybe two, three miles, tops. It was a nice day so she just yelled 'bye' and hopped on her bike and took off."

She paused and sipped a little water. Virginia rubbed her back.

"Later that day, when dinner rolled around and Donna still hadn't turned up anywhere, we all started to get worried. Mom called around to her friends. Dad got home and was talking to the police."

"What did you think?" I asked.

"Truth?" She cocked her head at me again. "I was pretty sure Dad had killed her."

"What made you sure?"

She shrugged. "A life lived with him?" she said. "If you had asked me that day, 'Who is the most likely candidate for killing Donna Dixon?' I would have answered 'Harold Dixon' in a heartbeat."

"Do you still think he did?"

She shrugged. She did a lot of shrugging. "Apparently he was teaching summer school until about three o'clock," she said. "That was during the time when Donna disappeared. So it appears that he didn't."

"Can you think of anyone else who might have? Who would have wanted to?"

"Kill my sister?" she asked. She shook her head. "No, I can't," she said. "Donna was a sweet girl. Everyone liked her. She was only 17. Who has enemies at age 17? No one." She paused. "I'm sorry."

"Don't be," I said. "You left home at what … eighteen?"

"Wouldn't you?" She fixed me with a cold stare. "I started working at fifteen. Any old job I could find. Part time. Here and there. Babysat my ass off, part for the money and part to get away from home. Saved every last dime I could. I was driven. When I finally had a thousand bucks, I up and left. Took a bus all the way to Los Angeles. As far away as I could get. Never looked back."

"How is your relationship with your Dad now?" I asked.

"Nonexistent," she said.

"Didn't you come home for Easter last month?"

"No fuckin' way," she said. Virginia, next to her, nodded in emphatic agreement. "He tell you that?" she asked. "Fuckin' liar."

I thanked the two women for taking the time to talk to me. I offered to buy them dessert, but they declined. When they left, Siggi gave Frannie a long silent hug.

CHAPTER 15

After our lunch with Frannie and Ginny, Siggi and I killed a couple hours at the Museum of Fine Arts, which had a Monet exhibition in one of their galleries. They had collected most of his studies of the Parliament building in London. We both liked his dreamy, almost unfocused work. I've never been a big art or museum person, but Siggi wanted to see it.

After we shared a pot of tea in the museum's cafe, I drove us down to the waterfront and we checked into the Boston Harbor Hotel. Our room had a lovely view of the busy waterfront and the jets landing and taking off from Logan, just across the water in East Boston.

Late in the afternoon we walked over to the North End to have dinner at Mare Oyster Bar on Hanover Street. The after-work crowd of Beautiful People was buzzing, but we still managed to find some seats at one of the firepit tables that made having cocktails at that place so interesting. I ordered a single-malt Scotch and Siggi had a glass of white wine, and we enjoyed the flickering flames in the center of our square little table while we stared out of the huge windows at the brick buildings next door and the looming towers of glass and steel that reached up into the misty skies beyond. Boston has come a long, long way from the rather dull, pedestrian, gritty and unfriendly city it used to be, long, long ago.

"What did you think about Frannie?" Siggi asked after we'd sipped our drinks. I had ordered a surf 'n' turf appetizer plate with braised short ribs, seared scallops and truffle mashed potatoes.

I was in the middle of a braised rib, so I waited until I gnawed off most of the meat and wiped my hands on a napkin before answering.

"Different perspective on Poppa Bear," I said finally. "Kinda jumps him up to a prime position on the person-of-interest list," I said.

"He does sound perfectly awful," Siggi said. "The mother, too."

I nodded and eyed one of the scallops. It was about the size of a silver dollar, grilled on both sides to a perfect golden brown. Siggi smiled at me and nodded to go ahead. So I did, popping it into my mouth.

"Of course," I said when I had swallowed, "We only have Frannie's word on what the home life was like in the Dixon house. Before I put Harold under 24/7 surveillance I'll want to talk to some of the other kids and confirm the story."

"Of course," Siggi nodded.

"And I'll probably want to talk to any of the neighbors who knew the Dixon family," I said. "Neighbors usually know if someone next door is an asshole. And I gotta check Harold's alibi at Portsmouth High School. Though I'm pretty sure the department checked that back in '91."

"What kind of teacher was he?" she asked.

"English, I think," I said.

"I wonder if there are any records at the school," she mused. "Parents or even some of the kids complaining about his treatment of them. I mean, if he treated his own children like he was a petty tyrant, it stands to reason he treated his students like that, too. At least from time to time."

I sampled a bite of the potatoes. I wasn't sure if I liked truffles. Hell, I wasn't all that sure what a truffle was. But the mashed potatoes had an earthy taste that wasn't bad.

"I was reading the old FBI psyche profile," I said. "It said that sociopaths like the killer in this case often behave and are perceived by co-workers, friends and even in some cases family members as perfectly normal. If that's true, then everyone else on the faculty at Portsmouth High back in 1991 saw Harold Dixon as just another guy. He could have been a *stern* teacher, or even a *demanding* teacher, but nobody would have suspected him to be a monster back at home, much less a potential killer."

Siggi frowned. "I don't know," she said, "I think if you are a bad person with your family, you are a bad person with everyone. I don't see how you can hide that."

I shrugged. "I tend to agree with you," I said, "But the FBI has all these psyche experts on staff. So I have to at least consider what they say might be true."

"Might," she said. "They could be wrong, too."

"And often are," I nodded. "That's why they call them the Fart, Belch and Itch guys."

The waiter came up and handed us menus. Said our table would be ready shortly if we wanted to think about ordering. I scanned the menu.

"Yum," I said, "Wild Boar Pappardelle. Can't remember when I last had wild boar."

"I remember you *being* a wild boar," Siggi said, her eyes sparkling with delight. "Have you ever eaten some?"

"Don't think so," I said.

I eventually settled for the pan seared salmon while Siggi opted for the lobster ravioli.

"You asked Frannie's birthdate," I said. "What sign is she?"

"Confirming my observation," she said. "Pisces are calm, strong, empathetic, in control and mostly unshakable. Frannie all over."

"Is there something I should understand about all that?"

She shook her head. "No, just that you can probably accept what she said as the truth. Pisceans are observant and usually honest. No BS, for the most part."

A couple of tables over, two twenty-something guys were showing off for their dates, wolfing down oysters on the half shell that had been brought to their table on a three-level metal tray. The guys were throwing back their heads and slurping down the little beasts while their dates were tittering and shaking their heads in pretended disgust. One of the young women finally agreed, after much taunting, to try one, to the aghast but fascinated interest of her friend. She managed to get it down and keep it down, to the laughter and approval of her friends.

"You like osyters?" he said to Siggi.

"Not really," she said. "If I was starving to death, I'd probably eat them. But if I have another choice … well, you can have mine."

"Sensible woman," I said. "Why you're a keeper."

Siggi smiled at me.

We moved over to the restaurant part of Mare when the dinner was ready. At the recommendation of our server, I ordered a bottle of Sicilian Nero d'Avola, grown on the steep higher slopes of Mount Etna. It was almost purple in color, tasted very fruity at first sip, but finished out nicely at the end with spices and minerals. It was a good choice with our food.

We were sipping coffee after the meal. Siggi looked at me. Something was on her mind.

"What was your father like?" she asked. "You don't talk about him much."

"To be honest, I never knew him," I said. "He went off to Korea when I was just a toddler and never came back. He was with the Second Infantry and was killed at the Battle of Bloody Ridge. We moved in with my grandfather, and he essentially raised my sister and me . With Mother's help, of course."

"Is there an unfillable hole in your psyche because of that?" she asked, a smile playing at the corners of her lips.

"I think you're in better position to know that than I am," I said. I signed the credit card slip and took the last sip of coffee. "Do I have defects? Disorders? Do I wake up screaming for my Daddy in the middle of the night when the moon is full?"

She shook her head. "Actually, you are the most sensible, grounded and giving man I've ever met," she said. "Which is why you're a keeper, too."

I reached over and touched her fingers with mine. "Thank you," I said. "Now if we hurry, we can catch the last few innings of the Sox game on the TV. They're in Cleveland tonight."

"Did I mention how romantic you were?" Siggi said. "No? Gee, I wonder why."

CHAPTER 16

AFTER WE GOT back from Boston, I called Daniel Horgan. He served as principal at Portsmouth High School for more than twenty years and I had known him pretty well for most of those years. The town of Little Penwick had made the decision in the 1960s not to build its own high school, but instead to send our high school aged students by bus over to Portsmouth. It was much cheaper that way, even with the cost of daily bus transportation, since we as a town didn't have to pay for a school building, along with the teachers, administrators and staff to operate it.

Horgan and I had many interactions over the years, both in dealing with truants and disruptors, and even in dealing with the good kids and athletes. So it had not been difficult for me to call Horgan and set up a lunch date.

We agreed to meet at a lunch counter called Reidy's over in Portsmouth. It's a smallish breakfast and lunch place with a long winding counter and a few plywood booths along the walls. When I got there, Horgan was already sitting in one of the booths, talking with some of the other customers in the place, many if not most of whom had been students at the high school when Horgan was the head man.

He was a few years older than me, but still looked to be in fighting trim. He had always been a little bantam of a man with a sense of tightly coiled insides and the kind of inherent authority that dared any teenager to try mouthing off with the promise that it would not go well. He had dark features, a strong face and was, as usual, impeccably dressed: jacket, tie, pocket square, cufflinks ... the works.

We shook hands and I slipped into the booth opposite him.

"You look the same as you have for the last twenty years," I told him with a smile. "I wish I knew how you do that."

Horgan smiled and shrugged. "Good genes, I guess," he said. "My dad had mostly dark hair until he turned 85. But you don't exactly look like you're at death's door, Haddock. Considering what they put you through."

"Oh, you heard about that?" I said. He laughed out loud.

One of the waitresses came over to take our order. Horgan asked for a BLT and some hot tea while I ordered a hot pastrami sandwich with fries and coffee. The pastrami was always good at Reidy's.

We spent a few minutes catching up. Horgan's wife had had some health problems in recent years, but was currently feeling better and doing well, he said. I told him about my winter of slow re-entry into real life again.

"We tried Florida right after I retired," Horgan told me. "Neither one of us liked it very much down there. Even in winter it can be hot and humid, and Priscilla about melted away. And everyone was so goddamned friendly, I began to miss the occasional angry remark or snarky backtalk from somebody. We decided we'd rather live in the cold and snow. Neither one lasts forever. And when you manage to survive the winter, it's like spitting into Mother Nature's eye. There's something rewarding about it."

"Can't say I disagree," I said.

The waitress brought our lunch.

"So, beside it being good to see you again, what brings you over to the island?" he asked as we began to eat.

"You remember the Donna Dixon case, thirty years ago?" I asked.

He thought about it while he nibbled on one corner of his BLT.

"Was that the young girl who disappeared when she was riding her bike to work?" he finally said. "They never caught the guy, did they?"

I nodded. "That's the one and no, we didn't ever catch him. Now that I'm semi-retired, I'm taking a look at some of the cold cases, and that one was first on my list."

"Were you on the force back then?" he asked.

I nodded. "Yeah," I said, "I was a newbie, but I was there. Anyway, I went through the old files and have been re-interviewing some of the principals, at least those who are still alive."

He nodded and smiled. "Glad that we're still in that group," he said.

I smiled back. "Fellow survivors," I said. "One of the people I talked to was Harold Dixon."

"Ah," Horgan said, "English Literature and Poetry. He might have taught English 101 for the freshmen a few years, but he managed to get assigned to the junior and senior classes later in his career."

"Anything you remember about him?"

He chewed some more on his sandwich while he thought about it.

"Good teacher," he said finally. "Dependable. Knew his material. Agreeable, for the most part."

"Most part?"

He shrugged. "Every year is different," he said. "Hell, sometimes every week is different. Teachers quit suddenly. Or they get sick. And you need someone to step in and teach an hour of American History or even Algebra. Some teachers will complain, try to convince you why they are the worst possible candidate to teach one class or another outside of their specialty. Some even start yelling for the union right away." He shrugged again. "Being principal is often like herding cats. Trying to get these supposed public servants to step up and help educate these kids. Some resist. Harold Dixon was usually quite happy to help out when necessary. Not happy all the time, but he did his part."

"The kids like him?"

"Never had any serious complaints, that I can remember," Horgan said. "He taught kids Shakespeare and Dickens and Twain and a few others. All the usual. All the basics."

He looked across the booth at me.

"You ever hear of the Rule of Thirds?" he asked.

"Don't think so," I said.

He nodded. "Education wonk speech," he said. "According to the Rule, about a third of any class will be engaged, interested, will respond to the material, ask questions, write good papers ... just a group that's into the whole learning thing, right?"

I nodded.

"Then, the next third of the class will be hit-and-miss. Some of them will get it, some of them won't. Some of them will try, some of them won't. Some will get it part of the time and just zone out the rest of the time."

He stirred some sugar and cream into his tea.

"Then there's the last third," he said, smiling. "These are the kids who can't wait to leave school for good. They want to go fix cars or shoot pool or smoke crack cocaine or have babies or whatever. Anything except sit in a classroom and try to read some shit by Shakespeare. We could save lots of time and effort if we just gave everyone in this cohort a D for Dumbass and told them to go away. They are not going to learn anything, no matter how brilliant the teacher is. Learning is just not in their DNA."

"The bottom third," I said. "I think I was in that group in high school."

He laughed. "I seriously doubt that," he said. "You made a success of yourself."

"Give most of the credit to the U.S. Army," I said. "Three years with the MPs in Nam made me grow up fast."

He nodded. "Whatever it takes," he said.

"So, did Harold Dixon agree with this Rule of Thirds," I asked.

"I think so," he said."But kids in the first and second thirds all bought into the whole education concept. The one's in the bottom third would be where your trouble makers were. They'd be the ones complaining about a teacher who's too hard or too mean or doesn't like them … things like that."

"And you don't remember any kids complaining about Dixon?"

"If there were any, I probably dismissed their complaints because they came from Group Three, the bottom of the barrel. I could have been wrong, but my working assumption was they were just trying to raise hell and once they left the program, we'd all forget about anything they once claimed. That's just the way the system works."

I thought about that while I finished my nicely greasy sandwich. It would probably be next to impossible to track down any of the kids from the lower third of Dixon's classes over all the years he taught school. Like Horgan said, they had long ago disbursed out into the wild to seek their fames and fortunes. Or misfortunes.

"Why are we talking about Harold Dixon?" he asked.

"I interviewed one of his kids," I said. "Who claims that Dixon was a perfectly horrible father. Cold, unsupportive, and on occasion, even violent."

"Oh, shit," Horgan said, wiping his mouth with his paper napkin. "So you are maybe wondering what might have happened between him and the daughter who was murdered."

"Harold had an alibi for the afternoon Donna, his daughter, went missing on the way to work on her bike. He was apparently teaching a summer school class that day. According to what he said, and apparently backed up by the school records, he was at the high school until about three o'clock that afternoon."

"Summer school, huh?" Horgan said, looking at me.

"Yeah," I said. "Why?"

His shoulders moved up and down. "Well, summer school is always kinda informal," he said. "I mean, it's summer, for one. Many of the classes held during the summer are the basics—math, science, even English and history—that are mostly remedial in nature. Designed for the kids who goofed off and failed during the regular school year. But they need the credits to keep going until graduation. And there are other classes offered in the summer for the general community as well. Many of those courses are offered at night, so working people can attend."

He paused.

"Harold's literature classes would be more designed for the kids who failed or need to add the credits," he said.

"So what?" I said. "If he was teaching class, he was teaching class. He still has an explanation as to where he was when his daughter was abducted."

"No, you don't understand," he said, shaking his head. "If you were a sixteen year old and you had failed Trig in the spring, you might have to come back for six weeks in the summer and take that class—an accelerated version—over again to get a passing grade and move on to Geometry or whatever the next fall. But if you got bad grades in English Lit or Poetry during the school year, you'd usually just take another elective course in the fall and move on. No need to come in for a summer make-up course."

"So he didn't have any students?" I sat up straighter.

"No, of course he did," Horgan said. "But the course he taught in the summer would have been much less formal and structured. They might spend an entire week just sitting around and talking about Hamlet or something. Or Dixon would send the class off to read some text or book and come back the next Monday ready to talk about it. Very informal and entirely up to the whims of the teacher. Unstructured is the word I'm looking for."

"So what you're saying is there might have been some days when Dixon was scheduled to be teaching a class of English students, but he might not have actually been there, in the classroom, actually teaching?"

"Exactly," Horgan nodded. "Happened a lot. It's summer. It's hot and sticky. Everyone wants to be outside, at the beach, wherever. Would you rather have five or six students sitting around in a stuffy, non-air-conditioned classroom, or would you assign them to spend a few days at home reading Jane Eyre or something and then have everyone come in the next week and discuss? Most teachers would prefer to send the class off to read and then go to the beach. Or the golf course. Or out on their boat."

"Or to Little Penwick to kill your daughter," I said.

Horgan didn't respond to that. He just looked at me, steadily.

"But the school told the investigators back then that Dixon was in the building that day," I said. "That was his alibi."

"It was summer school, Julius," Horgan said. "It was summer for the school administrators, too. They like to play golf and go boating when the weather is nice, too. You'd usually have a skeleton staff in the office in the summer and they'd have zero interest in keeping close tabs on either the students or faculty in the school. If you had called them up back in the summer of 1991 and asked if Harold Dixon was teaching a class today, they'd look on the printed schedule, see Dixon's course in English Lit was scheduled for Room 301 and tell you 'Yes. He's here.'"

"But he might not have actually been in Room 301 that day," I said.

"Correct," Horgan said, nodding.

"Is there any way to find out for sure?" I asked.

"Probably not," he said.

"Son of a bitch," I said.

DRIVING BACK TO Little Penwick, I was thinking that Harold Dixon's alibi for his whereabouts on the day his daughter disappeared had just been exploded. But it seemed there was no way to find out for sure where he had been that day.

Since I was out and about, I decided to stop in at Alma's Bakery, located in a tiny strip center near the Little Penwick town line, on the Long Highway. It was owned and operated by Alma Jefferson, a big black woman who had moved to town and started her business ten years earlier with her ex-Army husband Chester. After Chester had died from a heart attack, Alma had decided to stay and continue running her little one-counter bakery. Those of us on the Little Penwick police force were happy that she did, since Alma made the best donuts in southern New England, along with holiday pies and cakes and fresh bread almost every day.

I pulled in, parked and went inside and Alma's face lit up as if a Hollywood director had called for "lights!" She eased her considerable girth around the end of the counter and gave me a big bear hug. I was slightly concerned for my ribs.

"I was wondering when I'd be seeing you again, Chief," she said, holding me at arm's length and running her eyes up and down. "You are still too skinny by half. What they did to you is a crime all by its ownself, but letting you lose all that weight is even worse!"

"Siggi doesn't agree," I told her, "She thinks I should lose even more."

Alma made a *pshaw* sound that made her opinion crystal clear. She went back behind the counter, slid one of the glass doors on the display case open and reached in to grab two glazed chocolate donuts, which she knew were my favorite. With her other hand, she pulled out a square of waxed paper and put it on the countertop followed by my donuts.

"On the house," she said. "You need them."

"Thanks, Alma," I said. "How're you getting along?"

"Every day's a challenge," she said, hands on hips. "But the Good Lord ain't abandoned me yet, Praise his Name. But what about you? You get your job back with the police?" She pronounced the last work in the black vernacular. POH-LEECE.

I laughed. "I'm retired, Alma," I said. "My son is the chief now and they tell me he's doing a bang-up job."

"My, my," she said, shaking her head. "Little Gussie Haddock, chief of police. I remember when he and his friends would come in here and try to walk off with one of my gin-gersnap cookies. I'd always catch him in the act and then he'd grin at me and reach into his little pocket and pull out a dollar bill. 'I was jest kiddin' he'd say." She shook her head. "And now he's all growed up."

"Time passes," I said. "Things change. Way of the world."

"Do tell," she said, shaking her head in agreement.

The little bell above her shop door tinkled and we both turned to look. A slightly heavy woman with well coiffed, sil-ver hair walked in. Her make-up showed off her bright eyes and glossy red lips and she was wearing black slacks, a dressy white blouse and a black-and-white hounds-tooth coat. A big black bag was slung over one shoulder and she wore nice looking black loafers with two-inch heels.

"Hi, Alma," the woman said. She turned to me. "Well, well," she said. "Julius Haddock. A sight for sore eyes, Hav-en't seen you in ages."

"I was detained," I said. My line sat there in the bakery for a moment. Then both women began to laugh.

The woman came over and I kissed her cheek and gave her an affectionate hug. "Hi, Helen," I said. "It's good to see you again."

Helen Almy smiled at me, her face wreathed in pleasure. "You, too," she said. "Ben told me he'd seen you at lunch at Jack's last week. Said you were working your way back into life or something like that."

"Staying busy," I said. "Beats the alternative."

"How's Siggi?" Helen asked.

I assured her that she was fine. I suggested we should all plan a dinner soon, the four of us. She nodded. "Yes, we should," she said. "I'll look at my schedule, find some free dates and give her a call. We'd love to have you two over for dinner."

"Sounds great," I said. "You sound like you're busy these days. What are you up to?"

"Oh, this and that," Helen said, tossing her head back. She turned to look at Alma.

"Alma, dear, do you have any croissants today?" she said. "Ben mentioned this morning that he hadn't had anything from Alma's in a long time. Thought I'd surprise him at breakfast tomorrow."

"Got a batch just out of the oven," Alma said, moving her girth in the direction of the kitchen in the back. I noticed the warm wafting odor of fresh croissants right out of the oven.

"Get a dozen for me, too," I called as Alma disappeared in the back. I heard a muffled response.

"How is Gus doing with the department?" Helen asked. "I've been hearing good things around town."

"So far, so good," I said. "Kids got the smarts, of course. Came from me. And he has a lot of experience from his days with the Rangers. I think the town's in good hands."

"Good," Helen said, nodding. "I suspect you had a lot to do with his being named to that job. I think the continuity will be good for the town. Better than trying to break in a stranger."

Alma came back out of the kitchen carrying two square brown boxes wrapped in twine. She handed them across the counter and we both slipped some bills to her in return. While she was making change, Helen glanced down at her watch.

"Crap," she said. "I gotta boogy. Got an appointment I'm late for," She picked up her box and waved at Alma and me.

"Bye-bye," she said. "See ya later."

We watched her go.

"Does Miss Helen have a job?" Alma asked as we watched her get in her Volvo and pull out of the lot, heading south. "Nice clothes, hair all in place. I didn't know she worked."

"Don't think she does," I said. I had been thinking the same thing. "But I've been away, so don't ask me."

I thanked Alma again and took my box of croissants and my donuts and left. In the car, I ate one of the donuts. It melted in my mouth. I wished I had a nice cup of coffee from the Commons Cup, but that was a ten minute drive away and the second donut would be long gone by then.

I pulled out and headed south on the Long Highway. I had gone maybe two miles before I realized I was following Helen Almy's white Volvo which I could see about a half mile ahead. We came up on the intersection with Easterly Road, and I almost turned east at the corner, heading back towards my house. But I didn't turn. Instead, I followed along as Helen continued south before turning on Goodman's Road in another mile. I knew we were heading for The Heights, a long bluff overlooking the coastline where a line of summer places occupied the high ground above the rock-strewn beach below. There were more mansions across the road and others occupied expensive lots overlooking the Penwick Links golf course, whose fairways wound through the shale rock outcroppings and around the salt ponds near the beach. The Heights was our main summer resident area, which would be fully occupied between Memorial Day and Labor Day, and mostly empty the rest of the year.

Helen's Volvo turned left on The Heights road and then left again as she motored up Widow's Walk Drive away from the beach for half a mile and then turned into a private driveway that scooted up a short hill. At the end of that driveway was the Kilmartin place, a three-thousand square-foot Gilded Age place with cedar-shingled siding, elaborate archways, beautiful carved-wood windows and a round turret at the top. I couldn't remember if it had been one of the Kilmartin's who had built the place, but the currrent owner, Barney Kilmartin, was a partner in one of the big Wall Street investment banking firms. He had inherited the place from his father, who, if I remembered correctly, had inherited it from *his* father. Three generations of Kilmartins, at least, was enough for the locals to consider the house *the Kilmartin place.*

I continued past the driveway, turned around a few hundred yards on and came back and parked in a shady spot just off the road. I could see the driveway in my mirrors and anyone who came up the road would have to pass by me. I turned off the car and ate my second donut. Slowly, a bite at a time, trying to make it last. It had been years since I'd been on a stakeout, since one of the perks of being chief of police was being able to order other officers to pull the all-nighters. But I remembered all the years when I'd done stakeouts as a police officer, keeping a soda bottle handy for pee-breaks and trying to keep awake no matter what. Now, I looked over at the woods to my left and decided I'd just pee behind a tree if I had to go.

Helen had said she was late for an appointment. I wondered if she was meeting Barney Kilmartin or meeting someone at the Kilmartin place. Either way, I wondered what this was all about. As I had told Ben Almy, women of Helen Almy's age usually did not have sexual flings. Not that such a thing was impossible. After all, Helen was a human being and all human beings have sexual desires. Well, *most* human beings do.

I was thinking about that, and trying not to think about Helen Almy in that way, when a black Mercedes Benz sedan turned into Widow's Walk Drive and sped past me. I made a mental note of the license plate and was able to catch a glimpse of the driver as he went past.

It was a man. Long, silvery hair. Square chin. He was alone in the car. The Mercedes turned into the Kilmartin driveway and disappeared up the hill.

I glanced at my watch. It was 2:30. The perfect hour for a little afternoon delight. A bit of small talk, glass of wine, on to the main event and everyone gets home in time to fix dinner. Thinking like that made me uncomfortable. I started up the car and drove away. I felt a little dirty. I felt I knew something now that Ben Almy didn't. I didn't want to know. But I did.

Helen Almy had met a man. In a big, fancy, unoccupied house. In the middle of the afternoon.

CHAPTER 17

First thing the next morning, I called Dottie Adams, the police dispatcher. As usual, she was on duty and sounded bright eyed and alert.

"Mornin' Chief," she said. "You wanna know what I miss the most about your being gone?"

"I give up," I said. "What?"

"You always brought me baked goods," she said. "Every day but Wednesday. I never figured out why you skipped Wednesdays."

"Hump Day," I said. "Halfway to the weekend. That should be reward enough."

She was silent for a moment or two.

"That makes no sense at all, Chief," she said.

"That's cause it's Wednesday," I said.

She thought about that, too. "Chief, one of us is having an Alzheimer's moment, and it ain't me," she said finally. "What can I do for you?"

I laughed. "I need you to run down a license plate for me," I said. "I would call Buzz, but he has to keep Gus in the loop on everything I ask for."

"Got it," Dottie said, "You want this on the Q.T."

"Very Q," I said. I read her the plate number I had seen on the Mercedes sedan the afternoon before.

"Gimme a sec," she said. I heard her keys clicking on her computer as she accessed the state's DMV database and typed in the plate number. She began humming to herself as she waited, a nameless, tuneless series of notes that sounded like she was trying to whistle through her teeth or something.

"Got it!" she said finally.

"Great," I said, "Who is it?"

"Not a who but a what," Dottie said. "That car is registered to Julian LaFrance Fine Properties."

"No shit," I said.

"Nope," Dottie said, "No shit at all. That big ole Merc is owned by that big ole company that sells big ole mansions to millionaires. What a surprise, huh?"

"Yeah," I said. "Thanks for the info."

"Come see me some day," she said. "I miss your handsome mug."

"I'll do that Dots … promise," I said and we hung up.

I thought about the information for a minute or two. Julian LaFrance had carved out a niche for himself in the real estate world, specializing in buying and selling prime oceanfront residences up and down the coast, from Newport all the way down to Buzzard's Bay. Starting his company sometime around the millennium, he had quickly built a reputation as a fast mover, with a seemingly endless supply of rich people loaded with cash who were willing to snap up a big expensive house as long as it had an ocean view. And if you were an inheritor of one of those big piles, but didn't really want to spend your summers there, or pay the hefty property taxes those kinds of places generated, Julian LaFrance was the person you call to quickly unload it … for the right price, of course.

LaFrance had several offices, a small army of real estate agents and he ran full-page color ads showcasing his properties in all the local newspapers. Plus, he donated money to good causes and supported all the art and music festivals in the area whenever he could. All part of building his upscale brand.

There was one more thing about Julian LaFrance, I thought. He was as gay as Olde Paree. Outwardly, loudly and proudly. I was sure there might be a few people left in Little Penwick that might still give a damn about LaFrance's sex life, but most of us had long since moved on. But I now knew that, unless Helen Almy's sexual proclivities extended beyond the boundaries of the possible and the probable, she was not having an affair with Julian LaFrance.

Which was something of a relief.

Because it was Wednesday, I headed for Jack's place in Burr's Village at noon. Time for the regularly scheduled meeting of the boys. Er, men.

When I arrived, everyone except Ben Almy was there. I helped myself to the usual bottle of beer from the cooler and sat down next to the two other guys.

"Where's Ben?" I asked.

The others shrugged.

"He needs to get a hobby," Billy Church said. "He called me three times this week and then couldn't remember why. I don't think he's handling retirement very well.

"Well, he worked over at that Raytheon plant for what? Thirty-five years?" I said. "It can be tough when one day they say 'OK, that's it. Here's your gold watch. Go away now.'"

"Spoken like one who knows whereof he speaks," Harlan Bailey said.

"I'm not retired," I said, protesting. "I'm as busy as I ever was."

"How's that cold case going?" Billy asked. "You found anything yet?"

I shook my head. "Naw," I said. "It's slow going." I wasn't about to share any of the information I'd uncovered so far, not to this group. It would be all over town inside of thirty minutes.

The door popped open and Ben Almy came in, looking a little flustered.

"Oh, good, you haven't started yet," he said.

"Nope," Harlan said dryly. "The ptomaine poisoning has yet to begin."

We all laughed at that. And laughed again when Junior Hastings chose that moment to come out of the kitchen with his tray of soup and sandwiches for us.

Ben grabbed a beer and sat down. We all began to eat.

Billy Church looked at me. "Say, Jules," he said, "Are you involved in this year's Town Picnic?"

I shook my head and smiled. "Nope," I said, "And damn thankful I'm not. *Kee-rist,* the number of meetings I had to sit through planning for those things. Very glad to let Junior handle all that now."

We were talking about the annual Town Picnic held on Memorial Day weekend. It was a gala gathering for the town, held on the Village Green and involving a huge chicken roast, along with steamed clams, chowder, corn on the cob, potato salad and about six kinds of pies baked by various citizens. There were games, pony rides and an inflatable bouncy house for the kids; softball, horseshoes and other activities and plenty of time for sitting around and catching up on the town gossip. Naturally, the town council and any other local politicians would be out in force, glad-handing, back-slapping and baby kissing. The picnic usually began in the afternoon, local bands played during the dinner, and at dusk there were the fireworks.

When I had been chief of police, I was responsible for organizing, preparing for and patrolling the festivities. While no alcohol was served at the picnic, that didn't mean that none was present or consumed, and that often led to trouble. The kind of trouble a town's police force was charged with handling. So I was more than thrilled that my son, the new chief, would be sitting through all the meetings with the council president, the town clerk, the head of public works and all the others, and then making sure the department was staffed and ready to patrol the event and its aftermath.

"Why do you ask?" I said now.

Billy shrugged, "The town usually takes out a special rider on the liability policy for the picnic," he said. "It's a simple thing. Designed to protect the town in case lightning strikes or a tree falls down or the fire department truck accidentally rolls over someone's foot. It's pretty routine stuff, but I haven't heard from anyone about it this year. No biggie, but Memorial Day is coming up on us pretty quick."

"I'll remind Gus about it," I told Billy. "I'm sure it's in the works. Somebody probably just forgot to fax you the form."

We finished up out lunch and Junior came out with a plate of chocolate chip cookies. We all took one.

"Have any of you guys heard anything about Barney Kilmartin planning to sell his place?" I asked, dropping that little nugget on the table. If anybody knew anything, it would be one of the guys at this table.

They all looked at one another. Nobody appeared to light up, which was the first sign of someone having an inside scoop.

"Not a clue," Billy Church said, shaking his head. "Far as I know, he's paid his home owner's insurance up to date."

"That would surprise me," Harlan chimed in. "Barney is still on the young side. He has grandkids, but they're still small. I would have thought he'd keep the place going as a summer gathering place for a few more years, at least. Until the grandbabies are in college."

"And that place has had Kilmartins summering in it since the Roaring Twenties," Ben said. "That's a hundred years now. Only reason he'd have to sell that place is if he's in financial trouble. And last I heard, Kilmartin Brothers is still making money hand over fist."

"What did you hear, Jules?" Billy asked.

"I thought I saw Julian LaFrance over at the Kilmartin place a couple days ago," I said. "I just wondered."

"Julian La-Light in the Loafers?" Almy joked.

"The Great Gay Hope?" Harlan Baily said. They both chuckled at their gibes.

"Yeah, him," I said. "And you bunch of homophobes ought to be ashamed of yourselves."

"Julian stopped by the office a couple weeks ago," Billy Church told us. "Dropping off some purchase agreements for the insurance policies. Did you guys know he's in line to sell not one, not two but three million-dollar properties this year? I think that's a record for Little Penwick."

"I wish I knew where the hell all these rich people come from," Ben Almy said, shaking his head. "But Julian LaFrance sure knows how to find them. And get them to sign on the dotted line."

"I've heard he's growing his business lately," I said. "Adding new offices and people up in Bristol and down beyond New Bedford…Mattapoisett or someplace near there. So his business sounds like it's doing pretty good."

"Guy's a savvy operator, that's for sure," Billy said. "And he might as well take advantage of the good times while he can. They don't last forever."

"Hey, if the real estate business is hopping, that must mean the insurance biz ain't doing too bad either," Harlan said, nudging Billy's arm. "I think you should pick up lunch for us poor folk."

Billy grinned at him. "I wouldn't know," he said. "I let Marcy handle the day to day. I just show up when its time to hand out the bonuses and the annual dividend checks. Long as its bigger than last year, I'm happy to let her do her thing."

We chit-chatted for a few more minutes, over coffee. But I had already confirmed what I knew: Julian LaFrance was not only gay, he was a gay celebrity in Little Penwick and the nearby towns where he did business. I could rule out any possibility of Helen Almy having an affair with him. Which was something of a relief, but still didn't answer what she was doing with him in the middle of the afternoon.

Our lunch group broke up. Backs were slapped, bills slipped to Junior Hastings and we filed out. In the small parking lot out back, Ben Almy came up to me as I opened my car door.

"Got a sec, chief?" he asked.

I got inside and rolled down the window. I liked having something as a barrier between Almy and myself. "What's up?" I asked.

He reached into his coat pocket and pulled out a folded sheet of paper. He passed it through the window to me.

"I kept a record of Helen's comings and goings over the last week," he said. "Marked down every time she left the house and when she got back. Thought it might help the investigation."

I unfolded the sheet of paper and looked at it. Ben Almy the engineer had indeed kept a meticulous journal of his wife's movements for the past week. Organized by day, he had marked down when she had left the house and when she had returned. There were entries for every day except Monday and Tuesday. I noted that she had been gone for three hours on both Saturday and Sunday afternoons. I looked for the day that I had run into Helen at the bakery and then followed her to the Kilmartin place, and noted she had been gone from home for two and a half hours that afternoon.

"I really don't think this is necessary, Ben," I said.

"I have to know what she's up to, Jules," he said, his voice wavering slightly. "I have to know."

I looked at him.

"Ben, if you think something is going on, you should sit Helen down and ask her," I said. "I'm sure there is a perfectly good explanation for all this—" I indicated the sheet of paper he had given me. "You're just making yourself crazy with all this. It isn't healthy."

Almy straightened up and looked over the top of my car at the other guys, pulling out of the lot.

"I've got to find out," he said. "If you won't help me, I'll find someone who will."

I sighed. "OK, Ben," I said. "Don't do that. It's just a waste of your money. Gimme another week and I'll let you know what I find, OK?"

He reached into my car and squeezed my arm in appreciation. "Thanks, Jules," he said. "Thanks."

CHAPTER 18

I WAS BACK at home later that afternoon, reading some more old files from the Dixon case when I heard a car pull up my drive. I knew it wasn't Siggi, since she had said she was having dinner that night with her daughter. I waited and the back door opened. Gus Haddock walked in.

"Hey, Dad," Gus said. "How's it going?"

"Junior," I nodded at my son. Gus was wearing the chief's uniform—black trousers striped in gold with white long-sleeved shirt, epaulets and twin pockets and badge, without the necktie as usual. Gus hated wearing ties and only donned one for official ceremonial purposes. "You want something to drink? Cup of tea? I can make coffee if you want."

Gus looked at his watch, a little wistfully. "It's almost cocktail hour," he said. "But I have a meeting at town hall in about half an hour. Probably not a good idea to meet with the budget committee smelling like Scotch. But thanks, I'm OK."

"To what do I owe the pleasure of your company?" I said.

Gus eyed the stacks of files and papers on my dining table.

"I was wondering how you were doing with the Dixon case," he said. "Buzzy told me you had him pull some background checks on a couple Dixons. Learn anything?"

"Yeah," I said. "I'm looking a little closer at Harold Dixon."

"The father?" Gus said. "He was teaching summer school that day, wasn't he?"

"That's what he said," I said. "But Danny Horgan told me that record keeping in summer school is not foolproof. As it turns out, he could have assigned outside reading for that class and none of them would have been physically present in the classroom, including Dixon himself. I'm trying to figure out a way to check on that. It's a little tough after thirty years have gone by."

"You like the father for this?"

"His kids tell me that dear old dad was a bit of a monster," I said. "Cold, mean and violent. None of that stuff turned up the first time around. The kids and the wife might have been scared shitless to talk about it back then. I'm still checking with some of the other kids in the family on that. But if it's true, and if he wasn't over at Portsmouth High School that day, then, yes, he does warrant a second look."

"And Mrs. D is dead now, right?" Gus said.

I nodded. "The daughter I talked to said she was an alki," he said. "Sounds like she knew what a dick he was and drank heavily and regularly to shut it all out."

Gus frowned as he thought about this. "Well, that's interesting and all, but do you have any proof of any of this?" he said. "We can't go throwing accusations around without some definitive evidence."

I motioned at the stacks of paper on my table. "That's what I'm doing, Junior," I said. "I'm going through the evidence and trying to find the pieces that fit. Or don't fit. I know how investigations work, you know."

Gus nodded and smiled at me. "I know, I know," he said. "Is there anything I can do to help?"

"Yes," I said. "I'd like to access the VICAP database and look for any instances of similar crimes, both before and especially after the death of Donna Dixon. The FBI profilers all agreed that a crime like this is rarely a one-off. There's almost always a second, or a third, or even more kills."

"But if it was Harold Dixon, wouldn't he kill another one of his kids?" Gus asked. "Why would he branch out and start killing other people too?"

I looked at his son. "You want me to start explaining sociopathic behavior?" he said. "That's why I want to look for other victims. I'm assuming that somebody ran a check during the investigation of Donna's death to see if there were any similar recent cases that might be linked. But I want to check for any cases between Donna's murder and today. I'm looking for a pattern. And we have a thirty year time frame now. Might be interesting to see what might have happened since then."

Gus thought about that, rubbing his chin. I could tell he was not sure that what I was doing was a good idea. Lots of things could go wrong in a cold case investigation. Facts that seemed important now, might not have been so meaningful thirty years ago, and vice versa. And Gus knew we had to be careful about casting aspersions at someone like Harold Dixon. Even if his kids didn't like him, Dixon was a respected member of the community. You couldn't just start throwing accusations at him unless there was some hard proof to back it up.

"OK," he said finally. "I'll have Buzzy run the query. Those things usually take about a week, you know."

"I know," I said. "Been there, done that."

"In the meantime …"

"In the meantime, I have other loose ends to follow," I said. "I'm trying to get the other kids to sit down with me, or at least chat on the telephone. And Dan Horgan is going to try and find the names of the students who were in Dixon's summer school class that year. It's a longshot, but worth a try."

"Okay," Gus said. "Sounds like you've got it under control."

"Well, it's never under control, but at least it's moving," I said. "About all you can ask for at this point."

Gus nodded.

"Oh, Billy Church wanted me to remind you about the Town Picnic," I said. "He hasn't gotten the form for the insurance rider yet. Just wanted to remind you."

Gus nodded. "Yeah, Jessica is on that." He picked up one of the files on the table and glanced at it. Then he put it back down.

"Something else you wanted to talk about, son?" I asked. Which was obvious.

"The town council is driving me nuts on the budget," Gus said, sinking down into a chair at the table. "They're questioning everything. We've needed a new dispatch ops center for years now. The software is about fifteen years old, which means it's ancient. Dottie keeps the current system running with duct tape and chewing gum. But they're picking at every dime."

"Murtha helping at all?" I said, referring to Bob Murtha, the longtime council president.

"Not so I can tell," Gus said, frowning.

I thought about it.

"He's probably letting them run loose on you," I said. "Probably figures you need to get your feet wet early on. Normally, Bob keeps a tight grip on the budget. He knows the department needs that dispatch upgrade. But he wants the council to feel like they have some input. That means letting them ask a hundred stupid questions and questioning every last dime in the department budget. "

I paused and looked at my son.

"I'd recommend patience," I said. "Let them ask all their questions. Let them believe that they control the process. In the end, Murtha will decide what stays in and what, if anything, goes. He'll make sure that all the important stuff gets funded. The council will go away thinking they put you through the wringer but good. But you'll get the money in the end. I think they call that a win-win."

Gus looked rueful. "Doesn't feel much like winning," he said. "That goddam Bill Christy thinks he's a senator from Kentucky or something. What an asshole. And Louise Cox keeps feeding him information that he can cram up my butt."

"It's like they say, Junior," I said. "The smaller the issue, the more vicious the debate. Circle the wagons, make sure your information is accurate, and let them pound away. They gotta vote on something eventually, and Bob Murtha will make sure you'll get what you need."

"Yeah, I guess you're right," Gus said reluctantly. "Be easier to just shoot about half of them. But that's probably against the law."

"I dunno, son," I said with a big smile. "Might be justifiable."

He looked over at the counter next to the refrigerator. That's where I kept my bottles of alcohol.

"Maybe it is time for a sundowner," I said. "All this talk of budgets and city council twerps has riled up my blood pressure. How about a quick one, for the road?"

Gus laughed at that. "Yeah, I'm feeling my BP is on the high side, too. Pour away old man. But make mine on the light side. I still have that meeting to get to."

I poured some bourbon into two glasses, added ice and a splash of water and handed one to my son.

"Cheers, Junior," I said. "And welcome to the wonderful world of Swamp Yankee politics."

CHAPTER 19

Gus left for his meeting and I went back to reviewing files. The days were getting longer as spring continued to take over, so when I finally looked up, surprised to see it was dark outside, I glanced at the clock on my range and saw that it was nearly 7:30.

The phone rang and, looking down at the screen, I saw it was a call from John Dixon, the oldest Dixon son. I had left several messages for him over the last week.

"Julius Haddock," I said, answering.

"Chief Haddock?" said the voice on the line. "John Dixon here. Returning your call. I've heard that you're looking into my sister's case again. How can I be of help?"

"Thanks for getting back to me, Mr. Dixon," I said. I thought using a formal address would indicate respect, make it more likely that John Dixon would respond positively to my questions. "I'm going over some of the old reports and files from thirty years ago and just had a few questions you could maybe help me answer."

"I'll do my best," Dixon said. "Fire away."

"You were working away from home on the day your sister disappeared, is that right?"

"Yes," Dixon said. "Harvey's Furniture Barn up in Fall River. It was a typical summer job. Mindless physical labor with about six other guys. Harvey ordered in these kits of cheap particle board from China and we knocked them together, then shipped them out to his retail customers around southern New England. 8:30 to 4:30 with an hour for lunch. No air conditioning back then, so it was hot as hell in that warehouse. Sweated like pigs. I was still at URI, so I was just trying to earn some spending money."

"Sounds like the crap job we all had back in the day," I said.

"Exactly right," Dixon said with a laugh. "Crap job, low wages, and we loved every minute of it. We were finally adults, right? There was a kind of liberation in that."

"When did you first hear about Donna?"

"I got home that night around six," he said. "The guys usually went out for a beer or two after work. When I got back home, things were in an uproar. Donna had gone missing, mother was in hysterics and Dad was on the phone with the police. None of us slept much that night."

"Must have been awful," I said.

"I stayed home from work the next morning," Dixon said. "They found her later in the morning. Things went from bad to worse."

"Can you tell me how your father reacted to everything?" I said.

"Dad?" There was a brief silence. "He was concerned, of course. He called everyone he could think of who might have known where Donna was. All her friends, school mates, things like that. And he was on the phone a lot with the police."

"And your mother?"

There was another pause, a bit longer this time.

"She tried to hold it together," Dixon said, a trace of sadness in his voice. "It was difficult on her."

I paused, about to enter difficult territory.

"Some of your siblings have told me that your mother was … had a problem with …"

"She was a drunk," John Dixon said. "No need to sugarcoat it. She spent most of the last forty years of her life nine sheets to the wind. After Donna died, she got worse. I'm pretty sure Dad was thinking of sending her to rehab at one point. I don't know why he didn't."

"What about your father?" I kept prodding. "What was he like?"

"He was a cold hearted son of a bitch," Dixon said. He said the words calmly. Matter of factly. Not a hint of emotion. "He ran the household like he ran his classes. Everything on a schedule, everything according to plan. His plan."

"And if you deviated from that plan?"

"He'd let you know," Dixon said. "Either with harsh words, or a fist in your stomach. They both felt about the same."

"Can I take it you are not close to your father these days?"

Dixon sighed, the first evidence of emotion.

"We see each other a couple times a year," he said. "I stop by at Christmas to say hello, and I call him on his birthday. That's about it. That's about all I can take."

"What about your brothers and sisters?" I asked. "Were you guys close back then, before Donna disappeared?"

"Yeah, I'd say so," Dixon said. "We all kinda understood the hand we'd been dealt as a family, if you can call that a family. So we all had this feeling that we had to look out for each other a little bit. Mother was mostly worthless, of course. But we tried to help her as much as we could. And we had each other's backs when it came to Dad. One or the other of us was always getting yelled at, or worse, so the rest of us would help that one deal with it. We'd comfort each other, I guess is the best way to put it."

"Did you tell any of this to the investigators thirty years ago?" I said.

"I certainly didn't," Dixon said. "I don't know about the others. Dad took me aside before I went in to talk to the cops and gave me one of those looks of his."

"What look is that?"

"He had this death stare that he'd give you when he wanted you to know that if you went one more step, you'd be in for it," Dixon said. "We all knew that stare. So when I got that before going down to the police station, I knew what it meant."

"So you didn't tell anyone then about your mother's alcoholism or your father's violent attitude?"

"No, I didn't," Dixon said. "I don't think any of us kids told. We knew what would happen and we had been trained to obey."

"Do you think your father could have killed Donna?" I threw that one down, wondering what he would say.

There was a pause on the line. Dixon blew out a breath. Finally, he spoke.

"I honestly don't know, Chief," he said finally. "I've thought about that over these years. I thought about it at the time. But Dad was over at the high school that day, right? So it apparently wasn't him. But I've still wondered."

There was another pause.

"Another thing I never told them back then," he said. "I think my Dad was having an affair."

I sat up straight. John Dixon was right. There had not been one word of such an assertion in the old case files.

"Why do you think that, son?" I said gently.

"I saw him one day," Dixon said. "Him and the … other woman. It was in a grocery store up in Fall River. I had stopped in after work to get some snacks or something, and I saw them over in the produce section. They were all snuggling and kissing and being all lovey-dovey, y'know? Made me feel a little sick."

"Did you know who the woman was?"

"No," Dixon admitted. "But I guessed it was another teacher at his school. She looked like a teacher. I went home. Mom told us that Dad was working late that night, a teacher planning session. He didn't get home until around 11. I remember waiting up for him and looking at the clock. Fucking bastard."

"Well, thank you for telling me that," I said. "I know it must have been hard to do. But it might be helpful in the case."

"You gonna throw the book at him?" John Dixon said. "I think I'd like that."

"Too early to tell, son," I said. "I've got a lot more material to work through before I can come to any conclusions. I appreciate your honesty. I will let you, and your siblings, know as soon as I've assembled the evidence. OK?"

"Sure, chief," Dixon said. His voice sounded like he didn't believe what I was telling him. I wasn't sure if I believed it either.

CHAPTER 20

IN THE MORNING, I had just made a pot of coffee when Siggi arrived. She had a bag of cinnamon buns from Alma's Bakery, still warm from the oven, that fragrant aroma filling the kitchen.

"Those smell awesome," I said, giving her a welcoming kiss. "I'll make some eggs."

"Let's eat outside," Siggi said. "It's a really nice morning."

She went out to wipe down the table on the deck and set out the cushions for the chairs while I scrambled some eggs, tossing in a handful of grated white cheddar at the end. I spooned some onto two plates, added a couple of the warm buns to each plate and poured out two mugs of coffee. Siggi came back inside, took out a wooden tray and put the breakfast on it. I carried the tray out to the table.

It was a gorgeous late April morning. The sun was still climbing in the eastern sky, but the day was cloudless and the sun's rays were almost luminescent on the water flowing through the Rockies just offshore. Because of the way the tides and currents washed through the collection of rocky outcroppings, the sea bottom was scraped clear of kelp and seaweed, leaving nothing but sand and pebbles, so the water looked as aquamarine blue as any place in the Caribbean. Gulls floated overhead, keening in the morning light, ever alert for a clam poking out of the sand they could snatch up and drop on a rock or a paved road. Way offshore, a huge container ship, piled high with colored metal rectangles, chugged slowly across the horizon, on its way to Charleston or Jacksonville or maybe all the way down to Ft. Lauderdale.

Closer to the house, the rosa rugosas, beach roses, were leafing out in the early spring, sending light green shoots out to catch the sun. In the beds below the deck, the daffodils and tulips were sprouting. In another month, Siggi and I would begin planting the annuals: zinnias, snapdragons, salvia and others to bloom throughout the summer months to come.

"Gonna go out on a limb here," I said, holding my coffee mug in both hands, enjoying the warmth and feeling peaceful, "But I think winter is finally over."

"Be a while before it really gets warm," Siggi said. "That ocean takes a while to warm up."

We sat silently for some time, enjoying the morning.

"Speaking of warm, how's your cold case coming along?" Siggi asked.

I grunted. I didn't want to get sucked back into the real world. I was enjoying the sun, the ocean, the gulls … everything in this calm and protected little corner of the world.

"The Dixon kids all pretty much hated their father," I said. "You heard what Frannie said, up in Boston. I talked to her brother John last night, and he said he thinks his father was having an affair when Donna was killed."

"Is that significant to the case?" Siggi asked.

"Could be," I nodded. "Maybe Donna found out. Kids always know about these things, somehow. John said he saw his Dad with the other woman in a grocery store. Maybe Donna saw something too. Maybe she said something to him. That could be a motive."

"If Harold was the killer," Siggi said.

I nodded. "But there are still lots of questions," I said. "Was Dixon really at the high school that day? We don't know. Was he really having an affair? We don't know. And it all took place thirty years ago, which means memories are imperfect, witnesses have left or died, proof is hard to pin down."

"So you have hints, but not a clear picture," she said.

"Exactly," I nodded. "And certainly not enough to make a move. "

"What are you going to do next?" she asked.

"I've got a few more people to talk to," I said. "Two of the kids. I'll ask Dan Horgan about the affair possibility. Maybe he remembers something. Maybe he can help track down the woman, if there was one. He's also trying to find any of the students taking Dixon's summer school classes that year. A longshot, but you never know."

I poured myself another cup of coffee.

"And Junior said he'd run some queries on the FBI's database, see if there were any similar crimes before and especially after Donna Dixon," Julius said. "That's also a longshot, but stranger things have happened."

Siggi began clearing the plates, putting them back on the tray.

"Have you decided what to do with Helen Almy?" she asked.

I sighed. I knew that subject was going to come up again. Siggi would never attempt to tell me directly what she thought I should do. She'd just keep nibbling around the edges, poking and prodding until I finally did the right thing. Or what she wanted me to do, which often turned out to be the same thing.

"Yeah," I said finally. "I'm pretty sure I know what's going on. I just don't know why."

"That sounds ... interesting," she said. But she smiled.

"Yeah," I said. "Interesting."

SIGGI LEFT AFTER breakfast. I took a shower and dressed. Then I picked up the phone and called the local office of La-France Fine Properties.

"Good morning," said a bright and cheerful voice. "How can we help you today?"

"Morning," I said. "My name is Bob Smith. I'm down from Boston and in this area today and would like to meet with an agent to talk about some properties I'm interested in."

"Very good, sir," the voice said. "Let me connect you with Winston Cramer, one of our top producing agents. I'm sure he can be of assistance."

"That's very nice," Julius said, "But I was wondering if I could speak with Helen Almy. She's a friend of a friend and they highly recommended I talk with her. Is she in today?"

"I'm sorry, Mr. Smith," the voice said, "She's not in the office at the moment. Perhaps I can get your number and have her give you a call?"

"Yeah, that'd be good," I said. I paused. "No, wait, I have an idea. Give her a call and ask her to meet me for lunch at the Roadhouse. I'm going to be tied up in meetings all morning, but I can get there at 12:30." I read out a series of numbers that wasn't his own phone. "If she can't make it, have her call and we'll schedule something else. OK?"

"Certainly Mr. Smith," the voice said. "I will take care of this right away. And thank you for thinking of LaFrance Fine Properties." They rang off.

That done, I spent the rest of the morning on the telephone. I called the numbers I had for both Catherine and Billy Dixon, the last two of the siblings, and left a message asking for a callback. Then I called Dan Horgan again.

"Morning chief," the former principal said when he answered. "You just caught me. I'm going to get some golf in today while the sun shines."

"Good day for it," I said.

I told Horgan that one of Harold Dixon's children had seen their father with a woman and that there was a suspicion of an affair. He said that John Dixon said the woman looked like a teacher.

"Was there any suspicion that Harold might be having a fling with another teacher?" I asked.

Horgan sighed. "Chief," he said, "I gave up policing my faculty's sex lives many years ago. It's a fool's game, for one, and two, it almost always comes back to bite you on the ass, whether it's true or not. High school teachers are like anyone else. They have sex lives and sex drives and just like in any other workplace, people work together closely and collaboratively and sometimes they develop feelings for each other. My default position was to warn them not to do it, tell them what I'd have to do if it became public knowledge, and to stay the hell out of it."

"I understand, Dan," I said. "Same thing happens in a police department, even if we don't have quite as many female officers as you do female teachers. And like you, I tried to keep my nose out of people's private business. Unless it affected their work."

"Exactly," Horgan said.

"But this is a murder case," I said. "And if Harold Dixon was having a fling and that woman is still alive today, she might have some pertinent information. I owe it to Donna Dixon to find out what I can."

Horgan was silent. Then he sighed. "I hear ya," he said. "Let me think about it. Maybe I can call Virginia. She might remember something like that."

"Virginia?"

"Virginia Sutherland," Horgan said. "School secretary for about the last hundred years. She's almost eighty now, but still has most of her marbles in working order. I'll give her a call."

"Thanks," I said. "Hit 'em straight."

Dan Horgan mumbled something that I didn't quite catch. But I caught the drift and it made me smile.

CHAPTER 21

I PULLED INTO the parking lot of the Roadhouse Grill just after 12:30. I had deliberately waited a few minutes because I wanted to make sure Helen Almy arrived first. I figured that with a potential new customer on the hook, she'd be there ready to go at the stroke of the appointed time.

I walked in and nodded at Charley Clarke, the ageless bartender working the long wooden bar along one end of the restaurant. The other round tables and booths were mostly full. The nice weather had apparently brought out the customers today.

Scanning the room, I saw Helen Almy in a table for four in the far corner of the room. She was dressed in a smart business suit, and her hair and makeup were perfect. She had some La-France Properties brochures in front of her, and was looking at a sheet of current listings. Probably wondering which ones this hot new prospect from Boston would want to see.

I slipped into the seat opposite her at the table.

"Hi, Helen," I said, "Pretty day, isn't it?"

Momentarily confused, Helen quickly regrouped and smiled at me.

"Well, hello you," she said. "It is a gorgeous day, isn't it?" She looked over my shoulder. "Did you bring Siggi today?"

"Nope," I said. "Just me."

"Oh, well, it's good to see you," Helen said. She had covered the brochures and papers in front of her with her hands. "But listen, I'm meeting someone. Kind of a business thing."

"Oh," I said. "Are you working these days? Ben didn't tell me that."

Her face colored and she cast her eyes down toward her lap.

"Yes, well, I haven't told Ben about my new job yet," she said. "It's kind of a secret."

"I know," I said. I stuck my hand out across the table, as if I wanted to shake her hand. "I'm Bob Smith, your hot prospect from Boston."

Helen looked confused now. "What?" she said. "I don't understand."

The waitress came up to the table, pad and pencil at the ready. "You folks know what you want to drink?" she asked.

"I'll have an iced tea," I said. "You'd probably better bring the lady a Bloody Mary. She may need it."

The waitress nodded and went away.

Helen had regrouped. She was starting to look angry.

"What the hell is this, Julius?" she said hotly. Two spots of red had sprung up on her cheeks. Her fingers began to drum on the place setting in front of her.

"First of all, Helen," I said, "I want to apologize. I kinda got caught in the middle here, and it's a place I didn't want to be. But here we are."

"You called my office this morning?" she said, eyes locked on mine. "Pretended to be a customer? Set up this meeting?"

"Yes, yes and yes," I said.

"How did you know I've been working with LaFrance?" she asked. "I haven't told anyone, outside the people at the office who know me."

I reached into my coat pocket and pulled out my Rhode Island private investigator's license. I passed it across the table and watched while she read it. Her eyes widened and her mouth dropped open.

"You are a private eye?" she said, sounding surprised. "Have you been investigating me?"

"Yes," I said. "And not really."

She passed my license back and her eyes hardened. She began to look angry. "I think you'd better start explaining, Julius Haddock. And it better be goddam good."

"Your husband has noticed that you have been spending a lot of time outside the house," I said. "You've been going out at night, in the afternoons, on weekends. He couldn't figure out what you've been doing, and the excuses you've been giving him didn't quite add up. So when he heard I was going private, he asked if I'd find out what you've been up to."

"Geezus fuckin God," she said, exhaling loudly. "What did he think I was doing?"

I looked steadily at her. She met my gaze, and then her face turned beet red. It happened in the blink of an eye.

"No," she said, mostly to herself. "No way. He thought that I ... that his wife ... he actually believed that I ..."

"He didn't know," I said. "He thought the worst. That's why he asked me to find out for him."

She was shaking her head in disbelief now. "That goddam idiot," she said. "That goddam foolish idiotic jerk. After all these years, to think that he'd suspect me of …"

"I told him that, Helen," I said. "I told him he was being stupid. I told him that he needed to sit down with you and have a talk if he had questions. But …"

The waitress brought our drinks. I took a sip of my tea, while Helen pushed the stalk of celery to one side and drained half her glass of the Bloody Mary in a single gulp.

"But he's a stupid goddam foolish man," she said, wiping her lips. "Honest to Christ, I think he's losing his marbles since he retired. He doesn't do anything all day long. He works in the yard, he's dragged out his old stamp collection and works on that, he makes lists of home improvement projects he thinks need doing … Holy Christ, have you been following me around town?"

"No," I said, shaking my head. "I have not. Well, except once. After I ran into you at Alma's. I followed you down to the Kilmartin place. Parked outside and saw LaFrance's big black Mercedes roll in."

"I hope you didn't think I was having an affair with him," she said, and laughed a little, pushing back her hair. "Although maybe you should tell Ben that. I'd like to watch his head explode."

"That's when I figured out what you were doing," I said. "Lots of women your age work in real estate. Good way to make some money."

"Most of the women at the LaFrance offices are much younger than me," she said, somewhat sadly. "But they told me from the beginning that my age had nothing to do with my success. It's all whether or not I can relate to the customers, show them what they want, convince them they can't live without this property or that. Hell, I can do that. I did have to go to real estate school for a few months, which is why I was always leaving the house." She paused and shook her head. "And that idiot thought I was stepping out on him…"

"Why haven't you told him what you're doing?" I asked.

She drank some more of her cocktail. "Legitimate question," she said. "I was waiting for the right time, I guess. I've got two or three deals that may go to closing in the next few weeks. I guess my grand plan was to go home with my first big fat commission check and toss it on the table. He couldn't complain after that."

"You think he won't like the idea of you working?"

She nodded. "He's an odd bird that way," she said. "Gets it from his father. His father was adamant that a woman's place was in the home, raising the kids. He demanded that Ben's mother do that. She used to tell me how much she resented it. But she obeyed. I guess women did that back in the day."

"And you're hoping that when he sees how well you can do, how much income you can bring in, he'd change his mind?"

Her head fell, slightly, as if she suddenly realized that her plan might not be such a great one.

"Do you think he will?" she asked, looking at me with desperation in her eyes. "Do you think he will understand that

I want to work. I need to work. The kids are all grown up and out of the house. I can't just sit around and watch while he plays with his stamps and decides where to plant a hydrangea or two. I need something that makes me feel alive, useful. I want to do something."

The waitress came back and we ordered sandwiches. Helen asked for another Bloody Mary, since her first one was already gone.

"Helen," I said when we were alone again. "I understand why you want to work. And I am quite impressed that you signed on with the LaFrance people. They're pretty damn good at what they do. If you can sell houses with them, you should do very well, and more power to you."

"But ..." she prompted.

I shook my head. "No buts from me," I said. "I'm not your husband. Benjamin is. I'll give you the same advice I gave him. You two need to sit down and talk to each other. Honestly and openly. No more secrets. No more 'if I tell him, he might do this or that.' You guys are way past that. Time to put your cards on the table."

"But what..." her voice was almost a whisper. "What if he doesn't agree? What if he says no. I've worked pretty damn hard the last three months. Never mind the money I spent to go to real estate school. It's more than that. I don't want to give any of it up."

I shrugged. "We can play the 'what if' game all afternoon," I said. "Just like you could play the 'what if' game for the rest of your life. You've done something you wanted to do. Everything I know about Ben Almy tells me he'll be surprised and pleased. And supportive. Eventually. Once he gets over the shock. He'll certainly agree that what you're actually doing is a whole lot better than what he was thinking it was."

She nodded, her eyes watering a bit. She began gathering up the brochures and papers in front of her on the table.

"So what were you going to sell me?" I said, smiling at her.

"Depends on how much you wanted to spend," she said, smiling back across the table at me. "We've got some nice oceanfront places running around three, four million. But I'm about to get the listing on the Howe farm over off Easterly. That's only a little over a half mil. Five acres. Very nice."

"Is the Kilmartin place for sale?" I asked. "I wondered ever since I saw you and LaFrance meeting there."

Helen Almy laughed. It sounded like relief. "No," she said. "Julian wanted to show me the reno they did on their kitchen last year. I have another client who is thinking of re-doing the kitchen on a house they're interested in bidding on, and they wanted some ideas. Julian thought I should see Barney's place for inspiration."

I nodded. "Smart," I said.

The waitress brought their food, and Helen's new drink. We began eating.

"Tell me, did Siggi know you were spying on me?" Helen asked.

I smiled. "She knew that Ben had asked me to," he said. "And you will be glad to know that she advised me not to get involved, in the strongest possible terms. Over and over again."

"And you listened to her?"

"I always do," I said.

CHAPTER 22

Siggi came back over for dinner that night. I had bought some swordfish steaks at the fish place down on the docks at Little Penwick harbor, baked some potatoes and tossed a big green salad. And opened a bottle of a French Vidal blanc fume. She came in, looked at the fish ready for the grill outside and the rest of it and looked at me questioningly.

"What have you done?" she asked.

"What do you mean by that?"

She motioned at the spread. "You're putting on the Ritz," she said. "All my favorite things. That must mean you've sinned in some serious way and you're trying to atone."

I laughed. "Actually, Sig, this is a celebration meal," I said. "I've completed my first case as a private eye. Well, almost completed. I still have to talk to my client."

""So you're not going to spy on Helen Almy after all?" she asked.

I told her the story. How I had run into Helen, followed her down to the Kilmartin place, saw the black Mercedes come in, found out who it belonged to, and put two and two together.

"So I had lunch with Helen today," I said. I decided to

leave out the part of pretending to be a customer so she'd come meet me. That might set Siggi off again. "I told her about Ben's crazy ideas that she was running around on him. She was kinda mad about that. But she explained what she was doing and it should all be good."

"So, she's selling multi-million dollar properties?" Siggi asked.

I nodded.

She thought about that for a moment or two. "She'll be very good at that," she said finally. "Her rising sign is in Gemini and they have good communications skills. And they like change and challenge, which is what real estate sales is all about."

"She's also motivated," I said. "Driven, even, to do something useful with her life, now that her kids are grown up. But she's worried about Ben's reaction."

"I don't understand," Siggi said.

"Ben comes from the old patriarchal tradition," I said. "A woman's place is in the home. That's how his father was, so that's how Ben thinks it should be."

"How old fashioned," she said.

I nodded. "It is," I said. "But that's why she's been secretive about her new career. But she's about to close some deals, and she thinks when he finds out how much money she can make, he'll come around."

Siggi looked at me. "What do you think?"

"I think he's gonna hit the roof at first," I said. "But he's not a total crazed idiot. He'll come around."

She nodded. Which I think meant she agreed with me.

"I'll fire up the grill," I said. "You open the wine and bring me some."

She leaned over and gave me a kiss. "You're lucky," she said. "It worked out this time."

THE NEXT MORNING, I got a call from Dottie Adams, the police dispatcher at Little Penwick PD.

"Mornin' chief," she chirped. "Gus wanted me to call and see if you could come down for a meeting at around ten. Just FYI, it sounds important. He's calling in Jess Martin and Buzzy."

"Sure," I said. "Tell him I'll be there."

"You stop in and say hello, now," she said. "Or I'll come in and drag you out of that meeting by the scruff of your neck."

"Will do," I said and we rang off.

Three hours later, showered and dressed, I parked outside the public services building, shared by the Little Penwick police and fire departments, and went inside the half of the building that belonged to the cop shop. I nodded at Freddie Benes, the officer of the day, who was sitting in the bullpen behind the big glass wall working on filing the paperwork and was in charge of dealing with walk-ins, and went down the hall, pushing into the mostly dark dispatch room. Dottie was sitting behind her big computer screens, the light from the screen casting ghostly shadows across her face. I put down the brown paper bag that contained two scones from The Commons Cup that I had picked up on my way in.

Dottie's face broke out in a big grin, and she stood up to give me a hug and a peck on the cheek.

"Sight for sore eyes, Chief," she said. "And I'm hungry, too."

"Missed you too, Dot," I said.

I backed out of her office with a wave and went back into the bullpen. Buzz Franklin was standing at the back, coffee cup in hand, chatting with Jessica Martin, the lieutenant commander and assistant chief. They both waved at me. I was about to head for the break room in the back to get myself a cup of coffee when Gus came out of his office.

"Let's go, people," he said, waving his hand.

We all crossed the bullpen and entered the chief's office. My old office. I noticed that Gus had yet to change any of the pictures or posters on the walls. It looked just like it did when I was chief. Gus had brought in a third chair so we could all sit.

"I should send Siggi over," I said. "She could get this place looking better. Needs a little updating, don't you think?"

"If you say so," Gus said, a little gruffly. "Not that important in my book."

I shrugged and sat down. The other two officers followed.

Gus had some reports on his desk blotter, and he now passed copies around to the three of us.

"I got the VICAP back from Fart, Belch and Itch on the Dixon case," he said. "They moved faster than I thought they would. But they found some interesting stuff."

I was already halfway down the first page. I noted that Gus had asked the system to find and spit out any crimes over the last forty years that involved young girls being abducted, kidnapped, or disappearing without explanation. He had checked the boxes on the FBI form asking for cases that involved either homicide or assault. And he had asked the FBI computer geniuses to search back through all of Rhode Island, southeast and central Massachusetts, and eastern Connecticut. In other words, everywhere within about a sixty mile radius out from Little Penwick.

I flipped through the report and quickly scanned the next few pages.

The FBI's computer had discovered two similar cases. In 1997, six years after the Dixon case, a seventeen year old named Monica Morris had been reported missing after school in West Warwick, Rhode Island. She had decided not to ride the bus home that day, but had headed down to the local mall with some girlfriends, one of whom had a car. They had spent the afternoon hanging out at the mall, as kids used to do, fingering the clothes at The Gap and Old Navy and stuffing themselves with fries and sodas at the Food Court.

But when the girls had gotten ready to go home, sometime around 5:30, they couldn't find Monica. They couldn't remember if the girl had run off to the restrooms, headed down the mall to visit another store, or gone outside to sneak a smoke. But she was nowhere to be found.

It was several hours later before anyone got alarmed. When Monica had still not arrived at home at nine, her parents started calling around to her friends, and learned where she had been that afternoon. At midnight, they called the police.

Monica Morris was never seen again. Her body was never recovered. Her parents never heard from the girl again. The West Warwick police had eventually listed the case as 'Missing Persons—Possible Runaway." With no body, no one could claim foul play. The girl had simply vanished. Another forgotten cold case. Until the query from Little Penwick asking for cases where young girls had disappeared.

I flipped the page, aware that the others in the room were also reading furiously.

There had been another case, six years after Monica. This one was in New Bedford, Mass., the old whaling town at the head of Buzzard's Bay, about twenty miles east of Providence. This case involved a girl named Juanita Jimenez. She had been fifteen when she disappeared. She had left her home at about seven one night in March 2003 for a babysitting job with her cousin, who had two small kids. She had babysat numerous times, walking from her house to her cousin's every time, all without incident. But this night, somewhere in the quarter mile between the two houses, Juanita had vanished into thin air.

Again, the police had eventually been called. Streets had been scoured, friends interviewed, husbands and uncles polygraphed … all to no avail. The girl was gone. Again, no body had ever been found, no clues had been left behind. The parents had been devastated. The case had also been labeled "Missing—Possible Runaway."

I finished reading. I sat back in my chair, thinking.

"Three of them," I said. "Six, seven years apart. Different towns and states, also far enough apart that no one would remember or think to draw any inferences to what happened in the other place seven years earlier. That gap in time and place was probably deliberate. He knew what he was doing."

"All the girls have similar name patterns," Buzz Franklin said. "First and last name start with the same letter. Donna Dixon. Monica Morris. Juanita Jimenez. Do you think that means anything?"

"Dunno," I said. "Could just be a coincidence. Could be an indication of the perp's sociopathy ... he was looking for girls with those name patterns. I'm thinking coincidence, since the girl taken from the mall was probably more of an abduction event. I doubt the perp hung around and asked what her name was before he decided to grab her."

"No clues left behind for any of them," Jessica Martin said. "Only in Donna's case did the killer dump the body. He must have decided that was too much evidence to leave behind, and got rid of the victims in another way after that."

Gus made a noise behind his desk. "We can't assume that these three cases are related," he said. "All the similarities you just noted could be entirely coincidental."

"C'mon, son," I protested. "These three cases are by the same guy. I'll bet the mortgage on it. The time lapse between cases, the similarities in the names, similarities in the types of victim, the complete lack of evidence ...it's the same guy. Gotta be."

"We're going to need more work before I'm willing to go there," Gus said, shaking his head. "And I'm thinking this case may have just gotten too large for this department."

"It ain't the department been on this case," I said. "It's been me."

"Whatever," Gus said. "I'm gonna call in the feds. They've got the manpower to run down these other cases. We don't. There will be a hundred witnesses that need talking to again.

Plus more that might turn up. No, I've gotta call in the cavalry."

Jessica Martin was nodding. "I think that's the right call, chief," she said. "If this is a serial killer, and it looks like it might be, we'll need all the resources we can muster."

Buzz Franklin was nodding. "I think she's right, Gus," he said.

I was starting to fume. "What the hell," I said hotly. "I do all this legwork and now you're gonna take the case away from me?"

"It's not your case, Dad," Gus said. "It's the department's case, even if it was colder than a brass toilet seat at the North Pole."

"What about Harold Dixon?" I said. "I was beginning to build a case with him at the center. I've still got some threads out there that need to be reeled in. And now I want to know where he was and what he was doing in 1997 and 2003."

"Well, you can still follow up on some of that if you want," Gus said. "But once the mighty FBI comes in, they're gonna steamroll over everything you've done while they bring in about a hundred new agents. Analysts. Crime psychologists. You've actually done some excellent work here, taking another look at this case. I never would have queried the VICAP if you hadn't piqued my interest. I think we all owe you some props for doing some great shoe leather work on this case."

"Here, here," the other two cops said.

Despite the praise, I was having none of it. I stood up. I could feel my face getting red. "Screw you," I said. "This is my goddam case. You can call in whoever you want. I'm still gonna talk to some people, ask some questions. I'm gonna find this guy. And then I'm gonna bust his ass."

I stalked out of the room, slamming the door behind me as I exited my son's office.

But I took a copy of the FBI report with me when I left.

CHAPTER 23

I WAS STILL fuming when Siggi arrived late in the afternoon, bringing some bags of groceries in for dinner. She took one look at my face, which I'm sure was still red and angry, and stopped.

"What?" she asked.

"Junior is taking my case away," I grumped. "Calling in the federales. There are two other cases similar to the Dixon case. Two more girls gone missing."

Siggi began putting the groceries away. Meat and some fresh vegetables in the fridge, a carton of chocolate ice cream in the freezer.

"That's a good thing, right?" she said. "It means Gus thinks there's a case there. Which you helped uncover."

"It's my goddam case," I said. "He has no right to take it away."

She put some jars away in the cupboards, folded the paper grocery bags and stored them in the pantry. But she didn't respond.

"What?" I said. Her silence felt like disagreement.

"What was your goal when you started this?" she asked.

"Re-examine an old case and see if I could uncover any-thing," I said.

"Did you do that?"

"Hell, yes," I said. "And I've got a prime suspect in Harold Dixon. I just need a little more time to put all the pieces to-gether. He's the one. I can feel it in my bones."

"If it is Harold Dixon, what are you going to do?"

"Bust his ass," I said. "Put him in the jail for a long, long time."

"How are you going to do that?" she asked. "You are not a cop any longer. You don't have the authority to issue the man a parking ticket."

I had no answer to that. All I could do was sit there, fum-ing. She was right.

Finished with the groceries, she came over and put her hand gently on my shoulder.

"I know it's difficult," she said. "But things have changed. You've been a police officer for more than thirty years now. You were chief in this town for most of that time. You used to be able to snap your fingers and have people jump to do your bidding. But those times are gone. Now, you are the re-tired chief of police. You no longer carry the badge and the gun. That doesn't mean you are useless. Look at what you did with this case … you began looking at the old files, asking questions, digging in more than they did thirty years ago. You followed the evidence and you began to build a case. But now, you have to back off, get out of the way, let the professionals do their jobs. It's the only thing you can do."

I sat there, still fuming, the back of my neck red and hot. But, as I realized that her words made sense and were correct, I began to calm down. I've always been a realist. I've always always looked at the evidence and let those facts determine my course of action.

I exhaled. Loudly and deeply, emptying my lungs down to the bottom.

"Yeah, I guess you're right," I said finally.

She rubbed my neck softly. She felt some of my tension and anger begin to dissipate.

"Let me make you a cocktail," she said. "I'll make dinner."

A FEW HOURS later, dinner over, dishes done, we sat together quietly. Siggi worked on a crochet project while I re-read the FBI report for the third or fourth time, looking for something, anything, I might have missed. The telephone rang.

"Bill Dixon," said the voice when I answered. "I heard you've been looking for me."

"Yes, Mr. Dixon," I said, "Thank you for calling me back. I just have a few questions to ask you regarding your sister's disappearance."

"Why?" he said.

His response, brusque and slightly unfriendly, surprised me.

"Because we're still trying to find out who harmed her," I said. "You have a problem with that?"

"You people haven't discovered jack shit about Donna in thirty years," Bill Dixon said. "What makes you think it will be different this time?"

Mentally, I immediately thought *hostile witness*. That made me change my attitude and questions. I had to try and win him over. Make him understand.

"Well, memories are funny things," I said. "Sometimes, after years have passed, you remember something that seemed insignificant at the time, but which turns out to be important now. But you are right ... I could be barking up the same old tree. But you never know unless you keep barking."

There was silence on the line for a bit. Then I heard an exhalation of breath.

"OK," Dixon said. "I'll play along."

"Thank you," I said. I looked over at Siggi who was listening quietly to the one side of the conversation she could hear, working away furiously with her needle and yarn. I gave her a thumbs up.

"How close were you to your sister Donna?" I asked.

"She was my big sister," Bill said. "I mean, Catherine was my big big sister. She was the oldest. But there were enough years between me and her that we really didn't have all that much in common. Donna and I were much closer. Frannie too. John and Cath were one group and the three of us were another. We were just closer in age."

"I got it," I said. "Did you know all of Donna's boy friends?"

Bill laughed, a little uncomfortable. "Yeah," he said. "I was kind of a smart-ass kid back then. I used to sneak around, try to catch Donna making out and stuff. I mean, I was just a teen-aged boy, trying to figure out how all this boy-girl stuff worked, y'know?"

"You ever see her making out with Charley Stine?"

Bill laughed. "Oh yeah," he said. "They'd go down in the basement and snog around. They thought they were alone, but there was this closet down there, and I could hide in there and watch. They never did anything but make out. I mean, he'd try to grab a feel here and there but she'd always push him away."

"She have any other boyfriends beside Charley?"

"Not that I recall," Bill said. "At least, she never brought anyone else home for me to spy on."

"The medical examiner said she wasn't a virgin," I said. "Any idea who she might have slept with?"

"Well, if it wasn't ole Charley, then no, I don't know," he said. He paused. "I kinda remember hearing someone in the family talking about a mysterious beau she might have had. But I don't know who that might have been. Probably someone else at school."

"Did you ever see your father physically harm your sister?" I decided to throw that one down on the table and see what would happen.

There was silence on the line. "So someone's been talking to the coppers, eh?" he said finally.

I kept silent. Left my question to float in the air. And in his head.

"No," Bill said finally. "I never saw him hit her. At least, not with my own eyes. But I saw bruises he left behind. Many of them. On Donna, on Frannie and even John once had a black eye." There was another long silence. "Our father is not a nice person."

"I've heard that," I said. "I'm sorry. Must have been hard, living with that."

"Harder for Mother," he said. "She took the brunt of it. That's why she drank all the time. Only way she had to escape."

"Do you remember anything else from that time when Donna disappeared?"

Bill sighed. "It was surreal," he said. "I was just, what?—fourteen or so? I remember mostly trying to keep Frannie occupied. She was only twelve or thirteen. She didn't understand what was going on. She was like that deer in the headlights. I remember she and I played board games for hours at a time. One night, we never went to bed, just stayed up playing Clue or Monopoly or something like that. All night long. Mother and Dad never knew…they were oblivious. Weird shit."

"I can imagine," I said. "Anything else you remember?"

"Nah," he said. "It was all a blur at the time. People coming over, leaving food and stuff. Sitting with Mother, crying and holding her hand. I kept hoping it would be over, that people would leave us alone, let us get life back to normal."

"That ever happen?"

"The people eventually stopped coming," he said. I remember one night we all looked at each other and said 'Who's gonna cook dinner?' There were no more casseroles and stuff. But it never went back to normal, whatever that is. When Donna left, she took a piece of all our lives with her."

"Where are you living now?" I asked. "What are you doing for a living?"

"I live in Hartford," Bill said. "Own a small business. Landscaping, painting, roofing. It's a living."

"Do you stay in touch with your sister Catherine?" I asked. "I haven't been able to reach her yet."

"Cath? She lives out West somewhere. Denver, Phoenix, someplace like that. She's a CPA." He paused. "I really don't talk to my sibs much anymore. After we say 'hello, what's up,' there's nothing much to talk about except Donna, and I think we're all over that. Sad, isn't it?"

"Yeah," I said. "Sad."

CHAPTER 24

A COUPLE DAYS went by. Nothing was happening. I had tried several times to call Catherine Dixon, but only got her voice mail. I tried a few other ways to track down her location, but struck out every time. I didn't know if she had married or not, if she used another name or not, or even where she was living. It was frustrating, especially since I knew the FBI would be able to get her entire life story in about three minutes.

I also checked in with Dan Horgan again, but the former principal said he was still working on setting up a meeting with the former school secretary, so far without success.

So the investigation was at a standstill. At least, my part of the investigation was. It was frustrating, but I've been through countless investigations in the past and I knew this sometimes—often, really—happened. After a period of speed, when information came flowing in, there was often a period of quiet when nothing seemed to be happening.

Then, on the third morning, I heard a car pull into my drive, followed by the sound of two car doors closing. I waited and the bell on my front door rang. Since everyone who knew me knew to just come around to the back door, off the deck, I figured these visitors were strangers. I suspected I knew who they were.

I opened the door and saw two men who could not have looked more like FBI agents if they had been wearing those navy windbreakers with the gold lettering across the back that said "F.B.I." They were dressed in almost identical dark gray business suits, white shirts, ties, polished wingtip shoes. *They left the fedoras in the car*, I thought to myself.

"Mr. Haddock?" one of them said.

"I didn't do it, nobody saw me do it, you can't prove anything," I said. Then I stepped back and waved them inside.

They introduced themselves as Agents Crawford and Williston. Crawford was the older of the two, his closely cropped hair flecked with gray. He had a square face and a jutting jaw. Williston was younger, probably in his thirties, with reddish brown hair at a modish length and a rounder, more well-fed face. They said they were working on the serial killer case with the Little Penwick police and that the chief, Gus Haddock, had recommended they stop by and see what I could offer by way of help to the investigation.

"You guys want some coffee?" I said. "I just made a fresh pot."

Crawford demurred, but Williston said he'd love some. So I poured out a couple mugs, and got out the sugar and milk. Williston added two heaping spoonfuls of sugar and a dollop of milk. I, as always, drank mine black. We all sat down at the dining table, still covered with case files.

Crawford cleared his throat. "Chief Haddock…" — he paused, smiled, shrugged his shoulders— "…I mean, the *current* Chief Haddock told us that you had developed some information concerning the father of Donna Dixon," he said. "Would you care to share that with us?"

"What office are you guys out of?" I said. I felt like stringing this out a little. Yes, it was juvenile, but I was still resentful being taken off the case. *My* case.

"I'm assigned to the Providence office," Crawford said. "George here works in Hartford. What can you tell us about Harold Dixon?"

"Is Bill Devereux still the chief up there in Providence?" I said. "I've known Billy for at least twenty years. Good man."

"Yes, sir," Crawford said. "He says he's going to retire soon, but none of us believe him."

"Yeah," I said, "Always figured him as one that would only leave his office feet first."

Crawford paused, smiled again. "Dixon?" he said, eyebrows raised.

"Yeah," I said, figuring my delaying tactics had about run their course. "I went back through the case file in the archives." I indicated the stacks of files on the table. "Did the usual progression for a cold case. Talked to the officer who found the vic. He's retired now, living up in Fall River. His memories jived with the record from 1991. Then I turned to the family. Talked to the old man first. The wife died a few years ago. Again, his story matched with what he had said back then."

I stood up, went to the cupboard, and brought out a package of cookies. I brought it back to the dining table, opened it up and offered one to Williston, who took a couple with some muttered thanks. Crawford refused.

"But then I started interviewing the children," I continued. "There had been five kids in the Dixon family. When Donna was murdered, they ranged in age from twenty-two down to fourteen. I've talked to all of them, except for the oldest daughter, Catherine. She's apparently living out west somewhere and hasn't responded to my calls. Assuming I have the right number. It's been a long time."

Crawford was listening, and trying to hide his impatience. I could tell that he felt this visit to be a total waste of time. He was here just to keep the appearance of cooperation with the local police department in effect. I could tell by the look in his eye and the way his mouth was turned down at the edges, that he saw me as just a tired old man, over the hill, a rural rube who used to carry a badge and a gun and who wouldn't know a clue if it came up and smacked me on the lips. I figured Crawford saw me as a Swamp Yankee, even if he didn't know what that meant.

"Go on," he said, trying not to sound impatient. He failed.

"Anyway," I continued, "The kids all told me that their father, Harold Dixon, was a finalist for Worst Father of the Decade. They said he was mean, angry, distant and emotionally violent. Physically violent, too. They said that was the reason why their mother spent most of her adult life hiding in a bottle. They painted a pretty ugly picture."

"Being a bad father, unfortunately, is not against the law," Agent Williston said. There were a few cookie crumbs hanging on his lower lip. I watched as he licked them off. "What else?"

"Dixon's alibi on the day Donna Dixon was abducted and killed was that he was teaching a class in summer school over at Portsmouth High," I said. "But the former principal of the school told me that record keeping at summer school was hit-and-miss, and that it was not impossible that there was no actual in-person class that day. He and I have been trying to backtrack and find someone at the school, or in the class, that can remember. But we haven't come up with anyone, yet."

Crawford nodded. He took out a notebook from his jacket pocket and jotted down a note.

I decided to keep the claim that Harold was also having an affair with another woman, possibly a teacher at the high school, to myself. I hadn't pinned that story down yet, anyway. But I really didn't want these two guys stomping all over my case. There was plenty of other work they could do.

"And now, with the two new cases, someone needs to find out where Dixon was when those girls disappeared," I said. "I'd do it, but I'm told I'm off the case now that the heroes from the FBI have arrived."

"We've done that, Mr. Haddock," Crawford said. "He was teaching classes all day on the afternoon Monica Morris disappeared from the West Warwick Mall. And this was in October, not summer school, so his alibi is solid." He flipped a few pages of his notebook. "And when Juanita Jimenez disappeared in March of 2003, Dixon was attending a teacher's training seminar in Woonsocket, with about fifty other English teachers from around the state."

He flipped his notebook closed and looked at me with a flat, emotionless look on his face. "So it appears that Harold

Dixon is not our serial killer," he said. "Assuming that there actually is a serial killer."

"You don't think the three cases are connected?" I said, a little surprised.

"I'm not sure the other two cases are actually cases," Crawford said. "Without a body or any evidence of wrongdoing, it is possible that both the Morris girl and the Jimenez girl are still alive and living happily someplace else."

"Have you run them through the database?" I said. "Looked for records of their existence? Social Security numbers? Voting records? Parking tickets? Arrests?"

"Yeah, we did," Williston said. "Nothing came up." Crawford shot a quick glance at Williston. I noted a stiffening of Crawford's body and could see a brief shadow of annoyance cross his face. He hadn't wanted that fact to get out.

"So, two girls are still missing," I said. "Could be they've been murdered. Could be they're living the life of Riley somewhere where the FBI can't find them. What are you guys gonna do?"

"The investigation is ongoing," Crawford said, tightly.

"Uh-huh," I said. "You guys mind if I keep poking around a little?"

"Yes," Crawford said. "We *do* mind. This is now a federal investigation. We don't need some …"

He caught himself and stopped. I smiled.

"Country bumpkin? Flyover Freddie? Backwoods moron? That's the old FBI arrogance we all know and have come to love," I said.

Crawford stood up suddenly. His face had turned an interesting shade of red.

"Thank you for your information, Chief Haddock," he said. "If we need anything further, we'll be in touch."

Agent Williston also stood up. "Thanks for the coffee," he said. "And the cookies."

I held out the package. "Take a few more," he said. "For the road. Hungry work, being a G-man."

CHAPTER 25

AFTER THE FBI agents left, I sat there thinking for a while about my next steps. I had no intention of butting out of the case. But I knew I would have to fly low to keep out of the way of both the Little Penwick police and the feds.

I called Dan Horgan back.

"Hey, Chief," Horgan said. "I've got some news to report, but most of it isn't very good I'm afraid."

"That's OK, Dan," I said. "Today seems to be the day for bad news. What have you got?"

"Well, first, I talked on the phone last night with Virginia Sutherland, the school secretary for most of the last century," he said. "I'm afraid I was wrong when I said she had most of her marbles. Based on my conversation with her, I think a few have bounced out of the bag, if you know what I mean."

"Crap," I said.

"Yeah," Horgan said. "But if it helps at all, when I mentioned Harold Dixon's name, she had an interesting reaction."

"What was that?"

"She said, and I quote: 'He was a real asshole.'"

I said "So what? I've talked to a lot of people who seem to feel that way."

Horgan chuckled. "Yeah, but Virginia never once in her life used a vulgarity," he said. "At least, I can't remember her doing so. And she had to deal with some of the worst parents in the world, especially the rich ones who think their shit don't stink, and demand that you do something for their little Johnny or Janey or else."

"So she really didn't like the guy," I said. "Did you tell her to take a number and get in line?"

"You don't understand," Horgan said. "I figure with her advanced age, most of her filters have worn away. But in the rest of our conversation, and we chatted for about fifteen minutes, catching up, she sounded a bit like the old Virginia. Except maybe a little more forgetful, a little feebler than she used to be. But for her to use that term, it tells me that she really didn't like the guy."

"Well, that's interesting, but if we can't learn any more from her, I guess that's another dead end," I said.

"I suppose," Horgan said. "And here's another one. I checked in with the office at the school to see how far back computerized records go. I've forgotten when we put all student and faculty records in a database. They told me that it was around 2001. Any records before then are in paper format, and stored away in the archives in a warehouse down by the town dump."

I kept himself from groaning out loud. "So if I want to find out anything more about Dixon's teaching records, I gotta go dust-diving through the old records."

"Afraid so," Horgan said. "And to get permission ... well, that may well take some doing. With all the new privacy laws on the books, I'm betting they'll make you jump through hoops from now until the Apocalypse before they let you look at those records."

"Great," I said, my voice probably sounding as defeated as I felt.

"Now, if you can get a court order or a warrant, that might speed things up quite a lot," Horgan continued.

I knew, with the FBI's new information about Dixon's alibis for the other two missing girls, that getting a judge to approve a warrant to search the records would be a steep climb.

"Well, thanks for trying, Dan," I said. "I think I've probably exhausted the string on Dixon."

"Sorry I couldn't be of more help," Horgan said. "Let me know if there's anything else I can do. And let's do lunch again soon."

"Right," I said and hung up.

"Crap," I said. "Crap, crap, crap."

Then I picked up the phone and dialed another number. It rang a few times before it was answered.

"Frannie?" I said, "This is Julius Haddock down in Little Penwick. I've got one more question that you can maybe help me with."

I listened, nodded.

"I've been trying to call your sister Catherine," I said. "I haven't heard back from her and it's been a week or two. I was wondering if you had another number for her? Or maybe you could call her and ask her to call me back?"

I listened again.

"Thanks," I said. "It would be very helpful if I could speak to her. I appreciate the help."

We hung up, and I sat at my dining table, thinking.

This was the dead end part of an investigation. Most cases arrive here sooner or later. A beautiful theory about the crime has crumbled and there seems to be no way forward. A suspect you were convinced was the perp turns out maybe isn't after all. There's not much you can do—facts are facts, after all—but you've got to keep pressing forward. Someone out there did the crime. If it wasn't Harold Dixon, like I had thought, well, there's someone else still out there.

The problem was, I had no idea who that someone might be.

CHAPTER 26

THE NEXT DAY was Wednesday, so I drove over to Burr's Village to have lunch with the guys. I still hadn't heard back from Catherine Dixon and had not much else to do until I did. I was a little late, and was the last one to arrive. The other three were sitting at the usual round table near the window. I nodded to Junior at his usual place behind the bar and grabbed the usual bottle of beer from the cooler, and then noticed that my three friends were sitting rather strangely. Straight backed. Shoulders hunched. Hands folded. Not talking. No eye contact. Something was wrong.

"Gentlemen," I said as I sat down in the empty seat. "What's up?"

"You betrayed me," Ben Almy said, his voice low and trembling with emotion. "You had lunch with my wife. You told her everything. How could you do that to me? I thought I was your friend, you lousy no good son of a bitch!"

As he said those last few words, his voice rose in pitch and tone, so that he was almost screaming at the end. I could not take my eyes off Ben's face. His rage had twisted his features out of shape. His eyes had narrowed into pinpoints, his mouth was opening and closing like a fish tossed on the dock, gasping. His hands had balled up into tight little fists that were silently pounding the table. Droplets of sweat formed on his forehead. And, of course, his skin was a deep red shade. The shade of pure and utter rage.

I glanced at Harlan and Billy and saw that they, too, were engrossed by the sight of Ben Almy's rage. But they sat there, unmoving. As yet, they were not involved in this ugly scene. They both looked like they'd rather be anyplace else.

I shook my head, as if to clear away what was going on. "Ben," I said, trying to keep my voice low and calm. "I think you're reading this all wrong."

"Shut up!" Ben almost screamed. "You've ruined my marriage. You've ruined my life. You told my wife I was spying on her! How could you do such a thing? How?"

"I did nothing of the kind ..." I started to explain.

"Liar!" This time Ben did scream the word. The pain came from someplace deep down inside. Someplace that was dark and rancid. It made the hair on the back of my neck stand up. The other two men at the table sat back in their chairs as if they had been slapped in the face.

"I asked you, I thought as a friend, to find out why Helen was leaving the house so much," Ben said. "How hard can that be? You're the former chief of police, for God's sake. You would think someone with your experience would know how to handle something as simple as that. But, oh, no, you gotta take her out to the Roadhouse and tell her everything. You've ruined the trust we had. You ruined our love. Helen is probably going to leave me, and it's all your goddam fault."

"Now, look, Ben," I started again. But Almy was having none of it.

"Don't you talk to me, you son of a bitch," he yelled. His hands were trembling now. Almy tried to clasp them together in front of him, on the cheap place mat. "I don't want to hear it. Not from the likes of you."

I looked at Billy Church, silently imploring him to do something.

"Ben," Billy said, "Why don't you take a deep breath, get control of yourself, and tell us what happened? Maybe the four of us can figure out something here."

"What happened?" Ben said, still not in control. "I'll tell you what happened. My wife was stepping out on me. All over town. Sleeping her whore self around. Hell, she probably slept with all three of you bastards. So I ask my friend Julius here, once the chief of police and now supposedly a private eye, to find out who she was seeing. But did he? Oh, no. He did not. Instead, he took her out to lunch and ratted me out. She came home and read me the riot act. Told me to go sleep in the den for a few nights. My own wife! And it's all because of you, you useless sack of shit."

"Geez," Harlan Bailey said. "Was she really sleeping around?"

"No," I said firmly. "She was not." That made Ben sit back in his chair. "She was in the process of getting a job. With Julian LaFrance and his company. First, she had to go to real estate school for a few weeks. Those classes took up a lot of nights and weekends. Then she started tailing along with some of the other agents, including Julian himself, for the experience. To learn the business, hands-on, ground up. Also happened on nights and weekends. Julian seems to like Helen and thinks she'll make a good agent. That's why I asked you guys a couple weeks ago if you'd heard about Barney Kilmartin's place being on the market. I saw her and Julian go up there a week or so ago. As it turns out, Julian LaFrance was just showing Helen the new kitchen Barney had installed recently, so she could get some ideas for another client she's working with."

"Lies," Ben muttered, "All lies."

"Well, Ben," Bill Church said, "I'm pretty sure she's not sleeping with Julian LaFrance. Different teams, if you know what I mean. In fact, I'm pretty sure she's not sleeping with anybody, except you of course. She's been in my office a couple times in the last week. Picking up insurance forms for her clients. I think Julius is right. She's been studying to become a real estate agent."

"Well, that's gotta be good news, right Ben?" Harlan said, trying to inject some cheerfulness into the scene. "Hell, those agents that LaFrance has working for him pull down some pretty good numbers. I know Catherine Francis, over in Newport, she makes close to a half mil every year in commissions. Damn, son, that's BMW money."

"I'd get a Land Rover," Bill Church said. "More practical when it snows."

"The lunch is ready," Junior called out from the bar. "You want I bring it out or are you all still fighting?"

I waved for him to bring it. Junior went back into the kitchen.

We all looked at Ben Almy. His frame had seemed to shrink as we watched. His shoulders had slumped, his head was down. As they looked at him, his shoulders began to shake and we all suddenly realized that he was sitting there crying, silently. We exchanged glances, not sure what to do, if anything.

Junior brought out the tray of four soup bowls and a plate of stacked sandwiches. He, too, saw Ben, and he dropped the tray down on the corner of the table and went quickly back into the kitchen. Junior knew what to do: flee.

The three of us passed around the bowls of soup and handed out the cutlery and began to eat. Ben Almy just sat there, in his misery, shoulders shaking, head down.

"So Ben," Bill Church said, speaking softly and without rancor. "You seem to have a problem with Helen getting a job. Do you want to talk about that?"

Ben's head came up and he looked at Bill with reddened eyes. His cheeks were wet with contrails of his tears.

"No Almy man has ever let his wife work," he said. "It just isn't done in our family."

Bill nodded as he took a bite of sandwich. "I understand that, Ben," he said. "But, you know, it is a different age now. The way our fathers and grandfathers set up their households was one thing. Women in those days all stayed at home and raised the kids."

"Which is what Helen did," I said. Ben shot me an angry glance. Ben did not want to hear anything from me. But I wasn't going to allow Ben to insult me, especially in front of my friends. "And now their kids are grown, so she wants to find something interesting and challenging to do with her life. She wants to work, and the LaFrance job is made to order."

"Of course," Bill nodded. He had become the voice of reason at the table. "All our wives were pretty much the same. My Janice never worked, except for some volunteer stuff from time to time. But like you said, Julius, women today want to get out and explore the opportunities in the world. And there's really no good reason why they shouldn't. I mean, look at my daughter, Marcy. She went to URI, got her MBA at Bryant and came home to take over the business. That wouldn't have happened fifty or seventy years ago. But it made complete sense to me to let her run the family business. She was trained for it, she knows all our customers, and she's stepped right in without missing a beat."

"Betty was in the same boat as Helen," Harlan chimed in. "She wanted to work after the kids left home, but it was a little too late for her to go back to school. But she volunteers about three days a week down at the parish. They've got her doing all kinds of things, counseling kids, helping older people with appointments and meals, putting others in touch with the right departments in town that can help with their needs. It makes her feel like she's making a contribution, makes her feel good about herself."

"What's the matter with being my wife?" Ben said. "What is wrong with that? Why can't she be happy with what she's got?"

"I'm pretty sure she is happy," Bill said. "But that doesn't mean she doesn't have dreams of doing other things while she can. I think it's pretty impressive that she's had a goal, then went out and worked to get where she can fulfill that goal. Working for Julian, selling mansions to rich people? Hell, my hat's off to her."

Junior came out of the kitchen with a plate holding squares of spice cake. They were hot from the oven, still steaming and smelling of cinnamon, nutmeg, cloves and other spices. He put it down quickly and retreated back to his place behind the bar.

"Look. Ben," I said finally. "I'm sorry if I did anything to offend you, or to come between you and your wife in any way. That was certainly not my intention. I was just trying to help, the best I could. I mean, I didn't even want to do it. You insisted I find out what Helen had been doing with her time."

"Well, you helped all right," Ben said. "You did a grade-A fuckin' great job."

He stood up, looked at all three of us sadly, and walked out of Jack's.

We watched him go.

"Geez," Bill Church said. "Have you ever?"

"Never fails to amaze me how folks can get themselves all turned around, over the stupidest stuff," Harlan said. "Never."

"I guess this means I'm not getting paid for this job," I said. "My private eye business is off to a bad start."

We all laughed.

CHAPTER 27

SIGGI TRIED TO be as supportive as she could, later that night, but there wasn't much she could do. I gave her the blow-by-blow from lunch. She could only shake her head in sadness.

"I'll call Helen in a day or two," she said. "See if there's anything I can do."

"Don't apologize on my behalf," I said. "I didn't do anything wrong. Not my fault that Ben Almy popped a nutty."

Siggi shook her head. "Not helpful," she said. "This is a time when everyone needs to take a step back and reconsider our positions."

"Right," I said hotly. "I've reconsidered. I didn't do a goddam thing wrong. Ben Almy put me in an impossible position and then blamed me for it. Do not apologize."

She fell silent, but I could feel the weight of her disapproval.

"What would you have done different?" I asked her. "Ben was sure that she was out screwing around on him. That's all he wanted to hear. When he found out she hadn't been, had in fact been trying to find a good job for herself, he lost it. Completely. That's on him, not me."

"There might have been other ways to handle it," she said.

"Sure," I said. "I could have put a cap in his ungrateful head. That's one way to handle it."

She shook her head sadly, but that was the end of the discussion for the night.

IN THE MORNING, we arose, dressed, prepared for the day ahead. We were having a second cup of coffee when the phone rang.

"What?" I said, picking it up.

"Is this Chief Haddock?" said a female voice.

"Yes it is," I said.

"This is Catherine Dixon," she said.

"Oh," I said. "Thanks for calling me back. I've been wanting to talk to you."

"Yes," she said. "Frannie called and told me what's been going on. I'd like to talk to you as well."

"OK," I said. "How about now?"

"Now is fine," Catherine said. "I'm at the Commons Cup with my kids. Perhaps you'd like to come down and join me?"

"Be right there," I said. I hung up. "It's Catherine Dixon," he told Siggi. "She's at the Commons Cup and wants to talk."

"I'll go with you," Siggi said. "Help keep the peace."

She rode with me, in silence, as I quickly made our way across town to the village green, the triangular greensward with the Old Cemetery in one corner, next to the towering

Congregational Church, with other Colonial-era buildings rimmed around the three streets that formed the green. Behind the Church was a row of commercial buildings, including the Commons Cup, the town's breakfast spot, run by Betty Billingsly. I parked in a spot outside.

We both saw a tall woman in her fifties, with gray-blond hair pulled back in a bun at the back of her head, holding a to-go cup of coffee in one hand while gesticulating at the green to two children, a girl and a boy, who looked to be nearly teens. Catherine Dixon was tall, with a round moon face and a pretty smile. The older girl resembled her mother, also blond and on the tall side; while the boy looked to be maybe twelve or thirteen. He looked, as boys that age do, disheveled, unconcerned and gangly.

Siggi and I got out of the car and approached her. She looked up at us with a smile.

"Chief Haddock?" she said questioningly. I nodded. She stuck out a hand for me to shake. "Catherine Winchester," she said. "Used to be a Dixon. This is Rebecca and Gordon."

"Your brother Billy said you were living out west somewhere," I said, after greeting the kids. "You just get into town?"

She smiled. "Information within the Dixon family has always been a little mixed up," she said. "Secretive, even. No, my husband and I live down on the Cape, in Sandwich. He's a tax attorney and I am a part-time CPA. Busy as hell during March and April, able to pick my spots the rest of the year while I chase these two ruffians around."

She turned to the children who were standing there watching. "Why don't you guys go wander through the churchyard while I talk to the chief," she said. "There are some really old graves in there, from the 1600s on. Look for one for Elizabeth Peabody. She was supposed to be the first baby born on American soil, some time around 1645. Lived to a ripe old age and had about fifteen kids."

"Fifteen?" Gordon Winchester piped up. "She never heard of birth control?"

"Shut up, moron," his big sister said, giving him an affectionate little push.

"I'll explain later," his mother said. "Go now, and let me talk to Chief Haddock."

The kids ran off across the street and started walking up and down the rows of weathered stones, calling out dates to each other as they went."

"They look like wonderful children," Siggi said.

Catherine nodded. "They really are," she said. "Greatest blessing of my life. After my husband, of course." She laughed a little at that. It was a pleasant, soft laugh. She turned to look at me. "Would you like a coffee?" she asked.

"Thanks," I said, "But we just finished breakfast. Let's go sit on the bench over there." I pointed at one of the wooden park benches that were installed at intervals around the village green. We wandered over, and Catherine and Siggi sat down. I stood, propping a foot on the edge of the bench.

"Frannie told me you were looking into Donna's disappearance again," Catherine said. "She liked you. Said you seemed on the up-and-up. How can I help?"

"Well, there have been some developments since we talked to Frannie up in Boston," I said. "I had been thinking that your father looked good for the crime for a while, but I don't think it was him now."

"No," she said, shaking her head. "My dad was a lot of things, not too many of them very good, but I never thought he was a murderer. That would have been an entirely new level of evil."

"You weren't living at home when Donna disappeared," I said.

"No," she said. She was looking across at her children, still wandering up and down the rows of headstones. "I got away from that man as soon as I could. I had to wait until I graduated from college, since he was paying the bills. But the day after I got my diploma, I moved away. Packed all my worldly goods into one small suitcase and moved up to Providence with a girlfriend. Got a job at a store and never looked back. Hardly ever came back, either. I think Mother's funeral was the last time I was in Little Penwick. God, how many years has it been?"

Her voice had become softer, more reflective.

"Were you close to Donna?" I asked. "Before you left?"

"Not really," she said, shaking her head sadly. "We were almost half a generation apart in age. I was into college stuff, she was just getting into high school. I mean, we talked now and then, but no, I can't say we were best buddies."

"So she never told you any secret stuff?" I pressed. "Boyfriends, sex, any of that stuff?"

Catherine smiled. "No, not really," she said. "That summer, I knew she was kinda sweet on that boy, what was his name?"

"Charley Stine," I said.

"Yes, Charley." She smiled with the memory. "He was just a high school beau. He'd take her to the movies or to dances or to the beach with her gang. I doubt if they were sexually active. Times were a little different back then, but I really don't think she was into that kinda stuff. She was a good kid. She had plans for her future."

"The medical examiner found that she was not a virgin, though," I said. "No idea who she might have slept with?" I paused. "I don't mean to sound prurient, but knowing who it was might lead us to find whomever it was that killed her."

She waved her hand in the air dismissively. "No," she said, "I understand why you're asking. I'm afraid that I really have no idea. I'll bet Mother knew. But I guess we can't ask her, can we?"

"I thought Mrs. Dixon was mostly out of it," I said. "The other kids told me she was drinking pretty heavily most of the time."

"Yes," Catherine nodded, "She was. But that doesn't mean she was out of it. I think she kept pretty close tabs on all of us. Despite everything, she was still our mother. There's a connection there, a knowledge thing, that can't be broken. Even by a daily fifth of vodka."

Siggi reached over and took her by the hand. "That's very true," she told her. Catherine smiled at her.

"So there's nothing else you can remember that might be important?" I said, pressing on. I had hoped for the last Dixon kid, the oldest, to have remembered something that would give me a hook, an event, a person, a date.

"No," she said, shaking her head. "Afraid not."

I nodded. I was done. I had no more questions. There was nothing to go on. The cold case was still ice cold. I shrugged. That's the nature of police work. You dig and dig, you look for the weak spot and dig there harder. If you're lucky, you get a break. Something comes up, something doesn't quite match. You wait for that, you look for that, and then you move in hard. On the other hand, sometimes there's nothing there. I thought of Donna Dixon, abducted, stripped, murdered and dumped in a corn field. Sometimes there's nothing there.

"Are you going to see your father while you're here?" Siggi asked Catherine.

Catherine looked at Siggi and smiled. "Yes," she said. "I'm taking the kids over after we're done here. I think they deserve to meet their grandfather. At least once. I think they're old enough now."

She took a sip of her coffee and stared out across the village green, peaceful and quiet, the spring crop of dandelions springing up with their yellow dots all over the green grass.

"Then I am going to tell Dad, in private, that he will never see them again. At least until I am dead and gone. Maybe once they are adults they'll want to come see him. But I doubt it. I'm sure they will ask me why they've never met him before. And I will tell them. They're both old enough now. So it will be up to them if they want to have any kind of relationship with that man. But as long as its up to me, they will never see him again."

Siggi was nodding in understanding. "You said something a minute ago," she said. "You said that Donna had plans for her future. What were they?"

Catherine turned to look at me and smiled. "She was interested in becoming a cop," she said. "She was looking at the criminal justice program at City College Rhode Island over near Newport. I think she had even arranged to take a course or two over there during her senior year, to get a leg up for when she enrolled. She had talked with someone from the police department here in town who helped her make some contacts and get into that program."

"Who was that?" I asked.

Catherine shook her head. "I'm sorry, I don't know. Or remember. It was a long time ago."

"Yes," I said. "It was. Thirty years long."

CHAPTER 28

A couple of days later, Dottie called me and invited me to a case meeting the next morning at the police department. "Gus wants everyone updated on progress in the case," she told me.

"Good," I said. "I'll be there."

That morning, a front had blown in, bringing scudding clouds blowing in off the ocean driving cold rain and a chilly wind. Everyone who had been wearing short sleeves and shorts to catch the early spring sun had to go back into the closet to dig out the sweaters, long corduroy pants, woolly socks and even the quilted parkas one more time. April, as they say, is the cruelest month, and for good reason.

The meeting was scheduled for ten and I was right on time. I got there early enough to get myself a cup of coffee and a donut from the box someone had brought in, and made my way to the interview room at the back of the station, which quickly filled to capacity. Gus was there, of course, along with Jessica Martin, Buzz Franklin, the two FBI agents, someone from the Rhode Island Bureau of Criminal Investigation and me.

As chief, Gus took control and called the meeting to order.

"Right," he said. "Let's get an update. Crawford? You guys learn anything new?"

The FBI agent, impeccably dressed as always in his dark slate suit, nodded around the table to all of us. He flipped open a legal pad and reviewed his notes.

"We have definitively ruled out Harold Dixon as a suspect," he said. "His alibis for the last two victims were solid. He is still a person of interest in the death of his daughter, however. We dug out the records from 1991 that Chief…er, former Chief Haddock had alluded to, and it turns out that the week of Donna Dixon's killing, the English Poetry summer school class that Dixon was presiding over had indeed been assigned off-site reading. So he was not, in fact, at the high school the day his daughter disappeared. We also tracked down two teachers from 1991 who distinctly remember Dixon being friendly with a young woman teacher in the science department. They thought there were sexual connections between the two, but of course, that is just gossip. We are still trying to locate the woman teacher in question, but she has long since left the district. So we haven't been able to talk to her as yet."

He looked around the table. "It appears that Dixon may have been with this female teacher when the crime occurred," he said. "We will be able to pin this down once we've located the female in question. But we are discounting the idea that he might have been involved with the abduction and death of his daughter."

He flipped the page on his pad.

"There is not much else on the other two vics," he continued. "Our agents are backtracking through relatives, friends and schoolmates. But because of the years that have passed, it is proving difficult to find anyone with actionable knowledge. The investigation continues, but Washington has told us that unless we can shake something loose in a couple weeks, the case will be returned to the Open and Unsolved category."

"Back to the deep freeze," I said. "Great work."

Crawford shrugged. "I'm sorry chief," he said. "But that's how these things go. We don't have magic wands. We have to follow the evidence. And in these three cases, there has not been much evidence."

"To follow the evidence, you have to get out there and talk to people," I said. "It's out there if you know where to look."

"And you do, old man?" Crawford said. He tried smiling to mollify his harsh words, but it didn't work. Everyone in the room seemed to suck in a breath and they all looked at me to see if I was going to leap across the table and starting choking Crawford with my bare hands. I merely smiled at the man and nodded.

"OK," Gus said. "If that's all, then maybe we should …"

"Wait a second," I said, holding up a hand in a stop sign. "You haven't asked me what I've learned."

"Oh, boy," Crawford said, sotto voce. "Here we go."

"OK, Dad," Gus said. "What have you got for us?"

I stood up. "Few days ago, I finally talked to the oldest Dixon child, Catherine," I said. "Her memories were mostly the same as the other Dixon kids. Family life was hell. Mother was a drunk. Father was a cold son of a bitch. She got out of

Dodge as soon as she could and hasn't been back since, for the most part."

"Big effin' deal," Crawford said. "Wasn't there some Russian writer who said all unhappy families are unhappy in their own way?"

I stared at the man until he shut up.

"Catherine also told me that Donna Dixon had made some future plans," I continued. "She wanted to become a cop, or at least to go into criminal justice or law enforcement of some kind. She was planning to enroll at CCRI, which has a crim justice program, the following year, after graduating from high school. She had even arranged to take some introductory classes at CCRI during her senior year."

I looked around the room. For once, everyone's attention was focused on what I was telling them.

"There was somebody who had helped her in making these plans," I continued. "Someone who was in law enforcement at the time. Someone advising her, talking to her, helping her fill out forms and applications. In fact, it was someone working here at the Little Penwick Police Department."

"Son of a bitch," Gus Haddock said, exhaling the words. "Who?"

I looked at Jessica Martin and nodded.

"Julius came to me a couple days ago and asked me to research it," she said. "This department has always assigned one patrolman to work as a school and education resource officer. The duties include attending job fairs, school events, the occasional town school board meeting, and to be there to talk to kids, especially in high school, both to recruit new officers and just generally represent the department's public image with school kids. It's not like a big job in Little Penwick. Most of the time, the resource officer is asked to attend maybe two or three events a year, tops. No biggie, right?"

"Goddam it, Jess, who was it?" Gus said, voice on edge.

"Roger Hart," she said. "The guy who found Donna Dixon's body."

There was a general uptake of breath in the room. They all looked at each other.

"Based on that information," I said, "I did some more legwork. Y'know, like police officers are supposed to do. The second victim, Monica Morris, spent her last afternoon hanging with her friends at the West Warwick Mall. I went over there and looked up the mall's personnel records. Monica disappeared in the fall of 1997. Between 1995 and 1998, Roger Hart worked as a security guard at that mall."

I glanced over at Crawford, whose face had turned white.

"The third vic was over in New Bedford in 2003, six years later," I continued. "After he left the mall security company in 1998, Roger Hart was appointed as school resource officer in the Fall River schools, and he worked there until he retired. He was working there in 2003."

I stopped and looked around the room.

"I found a teacher at the middle school where Hart was working whose name is Jimenez," I said. "Same name as Vic Number Three. She's the girl's aunt. I called her yesterday. She remembers Roger Hart. Remembers talking to him about her own family over in New Bedford. So he knew about Juanita, how old she was, where she lived, all of it."

"Son of a bitch," Gus Haddock said again.

I tossed a navy blue covered report on the table. Everyone could see the gold embossing on it that said "FBI."

"We should thank our federal colleagues here for their contribution," I said. "This was the psych profile they put together back in 1991, thirty years ago. It says our perp likely had some connection with law enforcement or the military. The way the body was cleaned of any evidence, the clothing and any other traces of her disappeared forever. The spacing out of the attacks, both in time and distance from Little Penwick. The killer knew what we would be looking for, and he took great pains to remove them. Anyway, they were right. He was a cop. He was our cop."

"Let's pick him up," Gus said and the room exploded in activity.

CHAPTER 29

I'VE BEEN A cop for most of my life. I wanted, more than anything I had wanted in a long, long time, to ride out to Fall River in a squad car, blue lights flashing, siren screaming, to the quiet little middle class neighborhood where Roger Hart lived in his mother's neat little 1950s bungalow and storm in to put the cuffs on a serial killer.

But I didn't. Because I had also been the chief of police of my town for more than twenty-five years, and I had learned how to step back and let my men take care of the hard work of policing. As chief, my job had been to oversee, direct, support and encourage my men. Now, of course, I wasn't even the chief. I was an outsider, even though I still had a few inside connections.

So when the convoy of vehicles left the parking lot of the Little Penwick Police Department at high speed — the FBI sedan and the LPPD cruiser and the RI statie car — I stayed behind. So did my son, the current chief. We stood side by side and watched the convoy disappear down Meeting House Lane on its way up to Fall River.

"This is the hardest part," I said. "Letting your guys pick up the perp when you want to be there with them. You want to see the look on the man's face. You want to have the chance to shoot the sumbitch if he tries to run."

"Yeah, it's hard," Gus Haddock said. "Probably not as hard as telling parents that their teenage kid has just wrapped himself and his car around a tree late at night, tho."

"Different," I said. "Still hard, but very different."

"You think he'll talk?" Gus asked me.

I nodded. "Sure of it," I said. "He's been wanting to tell his story for thirty years now. He's probably proud that it took us this long to catch up to him. He'll love that part. He'll live on that when he gets to jail. Roger Hart, the serial killer they couldn't catch." I nodded. "He'll start singing like a bird, probably as soon as they put the cuffs on him."

"I just hope we can find the bodies of the other two girls," Gus said. "Those families need closure."

"Don't worry, son," I said, "He'll sing. Loud and clear and in gruesome detail."

Gus turned and looked at me, his father. "You did some great work on this," he said.

I nodded my appreciation. "It was police work, son," he said. "Piece by piece. Step by step. You know somebody has done it. You just keep asking questions the best you can until something falls out."

"Still, you did it," Gus said. "I'm proud of you."

I looked at him. "Thanks, Junior," I said.

"What are you going to do now?"

I smiled at him. "I have one more stop to make before heading home," I said. "One long overdue stop."

I drove over to Orchard Heights and pulled up in front of Harold Dixon's counterfeit Colonial. We were almost into May now, and the trees were budding out, the hedges putting on new growth. Dixon had a big forsythia bush at one corner of his lot, and it was a brilliant splotch of bright yellow blossoms.

I went up and rang the doorbell and Dixon came and opened the door. He cocked his head at me.

"What do you want?" he said. It was the unfriendly Harold, the one I had been told about by his kids and heard about from his co-workers.

"I have some news about your daughter's death," I said. "May I come in?"

He grudgingly stood back and allowed me to enter. He led me back to the den at the rear of the house, just as he had done when I first came to talk to him, several weeks earlier. But I knew a lot more now than I had back then.

He sat down heavily in his easy chair. "What?" he said again.

"The Little Penwick Police Department, along with the FBI and the Rhode Island Bureau of Criminal Investigations is making an arrest this morning," I said. "We found the man who killed your daughter thirty years ago."

"Who is it?" he asked. His eyes peered out at me from behind his thick glasses.

"His name is Roger Hart," I said. "He was a patrol officer on the Little Penwick force when Donna was killed. We learned that he also killed two other girls in the years after Donna's death, one in Warwick and one in New Bedford."

"He was one of yours?" Harold said. He smiled at me in an evil way. "My daughter was killed by a Little Penwick cop? That's an outrage." His hands had contracted into tight fists, which he beat softly up and down on the armrests of his chair. "You people ought to be ashamed of yourselves," he continued. "Why, I am going to talk to my attorney. Thirty years my little girl has been gone, and it turns out you people did it." He threw his head back and laughed out loud. "I am going to be rich when I finish with you, Haddock. I am going to be a millionaire."

I stood there silently while he cackled to himself, no doubt thinking about winning millions of dollars in a wrongful death suit.

"Well, before you start spending it, Dixon, you should know that if there is any kind of legal case that proceeds into court, we will call all your surviving children to the stand," I said. "They will all testify in open court about what an utter horror show of a father you were. They will talk about the times you hit them, especially Donna, and they will talk about the emotional abuse they suffered at your hands. They will talk about your poor wife who spent the last few decades of her life as an alcoholic and another victim of your abuse. And we will call the woman you were sleeping with, the science teacher, on the afternoon your daughter was murdered. So when you call your attorney, you should probably tell him that we will fight you tooth and nail, and we will win. Because no jury in Newport County will award a penny to a monster like you."

He glared up at me, defiant.

"Your two little grandchildren?" I said, "The ones you met for the first time a couple days ago? You start something with us and I will guarantee you never see them again, ever."

Harold Dixon sat there and turned pale and then red in the face. But he didn't say another word, just sat there and glared at me. I had nothing more to say, so I left.

I WENT HOME and began carefully packing up the case files stacked on my dining table. I put the files in chronological order and carefully packed them back inside the legal-size cardboard box from which they had come, out of the dusty archive room in the attic of the police building. The files would likely be needed for the coming trial of Roger Hart.

When I was finished with that, I sat down and called each of the Dixon kids, starting with Frannie. I told them that we were arresting the man who killed their sister. Frannie cried. Billy thanked me, over and over. John and Catherine were quieter, more stoic. But they too thanked me for calling with the information.

Siggi arrived late in the afternoon. Her eyes were bright with excitement.

"You should turn on the TV," she said. "They're going wall-to-wall with coverage. Police nab serial killer after thirty years and stuff like that. I think I even heard your name mentioned on the radio station. I was listening in the car."

"Whatever they say, it's probably wrong," I said. "Media people these days are morons. Back in my day, they had some real reporters. There was a guy at the Projo who would always bust my ass. But he went out there and talked to people on the street. He knew his stuff. I don't remember his name, but he was one of the good ones."

Siggi looked at me, shaking her head. "You're not going to collect on all the accolades, are you?" she asked. "You're going to stay in the background. Let Gus and the FBI take all the credit."

I laughed. "Well, the FBI will get credit for nothing, except maybe for their psych profile from thirty years ago," I said. "And I'm happy to let Gus get the good press. As he should. He's the chief of police and it was his department that made the arrest."

"After you took up the cold case and did all the hard work and digging," she said.

I shrugged. "You don't go into this business to take credit," I said. "You do it for justice. For the victims. I like that Donna Dixon can finally rest in peace tonight. She was the one I was working for."

She looked at me, silently. "That's the Taurus in you talking," she said finally. "Stoic, honorable, dependable."

I smiled at her. "Whatever," he said.

"Speaking of honorable, what are you going to do about Ben Almy?" she asked.

I sighed. "I don't know," he said. "I'm hoping he comes to his senses. Or maybe Helen can talk some sense into him. But he seemed pretty wrought up. I don't know if he can come back from that."

"I'm having lunch with her next week," Siggi said. "I'll see what I can do."

I put the last folder in the box and fixed the lid on top.

"There," I said. "My first case is done."

"How do you feel?" she asked.

I paused, thinking.

"I feel hungry," I said. "Starved, even. Like I could go for a T-bone over at the Roadhouse."

"Ooh," she said. "Can I get the maple-glazed salmon? I love that."

"You can have anything you want," I said. "Anything at all."

CHAPTER 30

About a month later, the residents of the town of Little Penwick gathered on the village green to celebrate springtime, Memorial Day weekend and an excuse to get together, break bread, let the children run wild for a few hours and catch up on the recent gossip after another long winter of being shut inside.

We call it the Town Picnic instead of the Rites of Spring, and it is a big affair where everyone in town gets involved. The civic clubs, the Lions, Rotary, the Elks, all volunteer their members to do something at the picnic. The Rotary guys handle the huge barbecue pits, cooking chicken on the 55-gallon drums cut in half and filled with charcoal. The Lions club guys staff the drinks station, handing out soft drinks, lemonade, iced tea and bottled water. Others police the grounds, especially around the two dozen or so picnic tables that are set out on the lawn, picking up trash and changing the plastic bags in the big bins placed around the green.

There are pony rides and a petting zoo with animals from local farms, including piglets, chickens, a few horses and even a couple of sheep which the kids enjoy, when they're not lined up to get into the big bouncy house where they can pretend they are weightless for a second or two. The Portsmouth High School marching band alternates gigs with our local junior high orchestra and a couple of local rock bands. This year, we had even some folk singers who came down from the neighboring town.

Over by the Congregational Church, there was a row of tables where groups and organizations could pass out literature and recruit new members. The Little Penwick Land Trust was threre, as was the LP Historical Society. The Senior Center had some of its members walking around and talking to seniors about the programs they offered all year long. We have a dedicated band of protesters in Little Penwick who pass out literature almost every weekend on the Village Green, on stopping wars, fighting climate change and other social justice issues, and they were all there enjoying the late May sunshine while they tried to convince the rest of the citizens of Little Penwick to join their cause. Or causes.

The weather was spectacular, as if ordered by the Chamber of Commerce: it was a cloudless May day, temperature hovering around 75 degrees with a light southerly wind. The folks from the Little Penwick Yacht Club, who were recruiting kids for their summer sailing programs, looked like they'd rather be out on their boats enjoying a comfortable reach down to Cuttyhunk and back.

Gus and I stood with Jessie and Buzz and surveyed the crowds. Everyone looked like they were having a good time. In addition to all the kids activities around the village green, the nearby athletic fields were also busy, as the town recreation department was overseeing some pick-up games of softball and soccer on the fields.

"Man," I said to the others as we watched people milling around happily. "You could squint your eyes and almost believe it's 1962 again," I said. "It looks like a community. One big happy family."

Jessie Martin laughed softly near my right elbow. "Until the kids over at the school break a window," she said. "Or until we nail somebody on the way home for driving and drinking."

"I know, I know," I said, "Even though it looks bucolic from here, I know this town, like every other town in America, is made up of individuals. They're all gonna do what humans do, and that's get in trouble from time to time."

"Which is why we're here," Gus said. "Try to keep 'em on the straight and narrow."

"Hey look," Buzz Franklin said, nodding towards Meeting House Lane, which came in from Main Road to the west. "Here come the politicians."

We all turned to look at the convoy of black SUVs with dark tinted windows. There were five of them. After the SUVs, I saw two TV trucks from stations up in Providence. This was an election year, and any politician worth his salt knew that the Little Penwick town picnic was a prime place for speech-making. We had set up a short stage at one end of the green and the speech-making was set to being at 3 p.m., in about half an hour. The TV stations had come to get a little B-roll for the six o'clock news: the all-American little town listening to their beloved elected leaders. Norman Rockwell would have been busy with sketchpad and pens.

One of our patrolmen waved the convoy into a special parking place and we watched as the doors opened and several of our elected officials got out of the cars. There were a half dozen or so security types who also got out of the cars, but they looked generally relaxed. The Little Penwick town picnic was not considered a hotbed of jihadism.

I watched as our Governor began strolling through the crowds, shaking hands and greeting people she knew. She was shadowed by an older guy with long gray hair who I think was the Lieutenant Governor. I couldn't remember his name, either because I was having a senior moment or because nobody in Rhode Island remembers who the Lieutenant Governor is.

Our Congressman, a small, balding man from Providence, got out of another of the convoy cars. He looked around and blinked in the sunlight. Even though he had represented our district for about ten years now, he almost never came down to Little Penwick. Probably because we were one of the few voting precincts in the state that uniformly voted majority Republican, a rarety in this heavily Democrat state.

And then I saw him: Preston Knox. He was talking with the guy I knew as John, his security dude, pointing at the people at the picnic tables. John nodded and began edging his way toward them. Probably looking for concealed carry gun owners or those who might want to do bodily harm to our attorney general.

I watched Knox as he conversed with the Congressman for a bit. Neither one seemed all that interested in pressing the flesh with the townfolk. Instead, they both stood near their SUV and chatted with each other.

"You aren't going to do anything, are you, Dad?" Gus asked. He had been watching me watch Knox. I guess he was nervous.

"Like what?" I said, "Shoot him? Didn't bring my gun today. I could go kick him in the nuts, but I think I'll pass. Siggi says Karma is getting ready to pay him a big visit soon. I'll probably just wait and see how that works out."

Gus looked at me suspiciously. He didn't believe me for a second. He glanced at his watch.

"Okay, it's time to get the speechifying going," he said. "Jess, you want to give me a hand?"

The two of them strolled across the green to the low stage. I watched as Gus plugged in the speaker behind the stage and connected the microphone wire. He went up to the mic, turned it on and said "Test, test," into it. The sound reverberated around the green.

"Right, okay folks," Gus said into the mic. "As the new kid on the block around here, it's fallen to me to emcee our speakers this afternoon." There was a tittering from the people on the green. "So let's get started. Our first guest needs no introduction from me or anyone else. She's been our Governor for the last eight years and has done a great job for the state. Ladies and gentlemen, please welcome, Governor Gina Rooney!"

There was lukewarm applause. Partly because a lot of the people in town were Republicans. Partly because people were still chowing down on the barbecue chicken and all the fixings, and their hands were already in use. Partly because down here, we don't do a lot of hero worship, especially for politicians.

Nevertheless, the governor got up and made a nice speech. Her second term was ending this year, but there was talk she might take a shot at the Senate seat in two years. So she talked about her accomplishments and how proud she was to have served the people of Rhode Island. Most people felt she had done a pretty good job as the first woman elected as Governor. She hadn't been particularly partisan and had tried to corral the state legislature into doing one or two things of benefit to the state as a whole.

They didn't bother to introduce the Lieutenant Governor for a speech. His term was over next January, too, and he wasn't running for the top job. And as a famous senator once said about the job of Vice President, "it ain't worth a pitcher of warm spit." The job of Lieutenant Governor is worth less than that.

Gus introduced the Congressman next, and he was greeted with a smattering of boos. Big city guy, Democrat and one who never showed up in town anyway, that was to be expected. But he gamely worked his way through a campaign speech which went on and on until he finally said, "And in closing ..." which got the biggest applause of the speech. We're a tough crowd.

When the Congressman was finished, Gus stepped up to the mic again.

"We have one more speaker today, folks," he said, "But before I bring him up, I just wanted to say something. I've been your chief of police for just about one year now, and I wanted all of you to know that it has been the honor of my life to serve this town. The men and women of the Little Penwick police department, along with our fire department crews and EMTs, do a great job serving and protecting the people of this town, and I am proud to be their chief. They make me look good each and every day."

He paused, and there was a wave of applause from across the village green.

"I also want to acknowledge, here and now, the fine police work accomplished by my Dad, your former chief of police, in taking up a thirty year old case, doing the due diligence and step-by-step police work that resulted in the successful arrest of a serial killer. That case sat in our files for decades until Julius Haddock stepped forward and helped solve the case. I just think we should all be appreciative of my Dad's dedication and professionalism. All of us on the Little Penwick police force think of him as a cop's cop, and he proved that to be true with his work on the Dixon case."

This time there was sustained applause all across the green; People turned to look at me, and I gave a little wave of thanks.

"So now, let me bring up to the stage our attorney general, Preston Knox. He is the man who decided to put my father in jail a year ago. Maybe he can explain what the hell he was thinking when he did so. Ladies and gentlemen, Attorney General Knox."

The Congressman had received a smattering of boos. Preston Knox got bellows, catcalls, fist waving, screams calling for him to resign and everything right up to and just short of rotten tomatoes hurled through the air. I noticed the TV cameras were filming the crowds vociferous reactions before they turned to show him taking the stage.

Knox had to stand there for at least four minutes while the boos echoed across the village green. It was glorious.

"Thank you, thanks," he finally said, when the sound slowly faded away. "Thank you Chief Haddock for your introduction. I'm not sure I agree with everything you said, but ..."

That set off another wall of sounds of disapproval, which again lasted for several minutes. The TV cameras kept running.

"I'm happy to be down here in Little Penwick," Knox gamely tried to keep going. "This is an historic town in Rhode Island and it's great to see so many of you here today."

"Shut up and leave," someone shouted from the crowd. Other people cheered.

Knox rocked back on his heels and then bent forward to speak again.

"Now, there's no reason to be rude," he said.

"Yes there is," came a woman's shrill voice. "You're a corrupt asshole!" The cheers grew louder.

It started slowly after that. At first, I couldn't tell what they were saying. But slowly, as more people heard what some were chanting, they took up the words. Others began pounding on the tables in time. Others were clapping. Soon, everyone at the picnic was chanting the words.

Bye-Bye Knox, they said. The chant grew louder and louder, the table banging made the plates and cups jump. People stood up and began screaming the words.

Bye-Bye Knox. Bye-Bye Knox.

At the podium, Preston Knox stood looking out at the crowd. His face was impassive, even though one could tell he was devastated. Finally, he shook his head, waved weakly and walked off. The chanting continued while he walked over to the row of SUVs and got inside his. John the security guy followed Knox, jumped in behind the wheel and the SUV took off back down Meeting House Lane.

THE REST OF the afternoon, people came up to me to shake my hand or pat me on the back. Many had kind words to say to me. I had a lot of trouble saying anything back to them. My voice seemed to have stopped working.

Somewhere along the way, Siggi came up and took my hand, and walked with me through the crowds of well wishers. She looked proud and happy. We made our way from group to group, greeting old friends and meeting new residents. Billy Church was there with his wife and daughter. Harlan Bailey came over to say hello. I even saw Junior Hastings, in his bib overalls, enjoying a chicken dinner with his wife and some other friends.

I felt a hesitant tap on my shoulder at one point and turned around. Ben and Helen Almy stood there. She was smiling brightly, while he looked slightly abashed.

"Oh, Julius," Helen said, "That was magnificent! And I'm so glad you can see how everyone in town feels about you after all that's happened."

I gave her a kiss on the cheek. "Thanks, Helen," I said. And I meant it. I looked at Ben, who was having a little trouble meeting my eyes.

"So how are you guys doing?" I asked.

"We're good," Ben said in a thin voice. "Working things out." He looked down at the ground, and then finally brought his eyes up to meet mine. "I think I owe you an apology," he said. "I was a bit out of line. More than a bit, actually."

I reached over and squeezed his shoulder. "Don't give it a minute's thought," I said. "We all go off the rails from time to time. Part of the human condition. Important thing is to treat one another with kindness."

Ben's looked even more abashed, but he nodded his thanks to me, took Helen's hand and led her away.

Siggi leaned in as they left. "Helen says they're talking a lot more than they ever have," she said. "She thinks he's beginning to warm up to the idea of her working."

"She made any sales yet?" I asked.

Siggi smiled and nodded. "Two so far," she said. "Pretty nice commissions on both. Which no doubt helped convince Ben that having his wife work in the real estate business isn't all that bad."

I nodded. "Good," I said. "Glad to hear it." And I meant it.

I saw my son come walking towards us, from about fifty yards away. He was talking on the phone to someone. He looked concerned. When he came up to us, he ended the call.

"Something wrong?" I asked.

"Maybe," he said. "That was a guy I know at ICE. They've got a report that someone on the watch list might have been seen entering the country in Miami." He looked at me. "They think it's Janine Stone."

"Might have been seen?" I said. "What the hell does that mean?"

"She came in under a new name," he said. "From Mexico. But facial recognition picked her up at Customs. It sure looks like her, they said. They're trying to find out where she went."

"She'll be back up here," I said. "She's got unfinished business."

"Yeah," Gus said. "That's what I'm afraid of."

ABOUT THE AUTHOR

James Y. Bartlett is an American journalist, writer, editor and author.

For most of his career, Bartlett worked in magazine journalism, specializing in covering the worlds of travel, golf and upscale lifestyle. He worked on staff as an editor with *Golfweek*, *Caribbean Travel & Life* and *Luxury Golf* magazines, among others.

But he also published hundreds of freelance pieces in publications ranging from *Bon Appetit* to *Esquire*, *Men's Journal* to *Golf for Women*.

Bartlett was the golf columnist for *Forbes FYI* magazine for the first fifteen years of that publication's history and wrote a similar column for nearly 20 years on the golf lifestyle for *Hemispheres*, the in-flight publication of United Airlines, the latter under the pseudonym of "A.G. Pollard Jr."

He began writing his popular Hacker Golf Mystery series in 1991 with the publication of *Death is a Two-Stroke Penalty* (St. Martin's Press). That series, now published by Yeoman House, contains seven novels. In 2021, he published *Year of the Sheep: A Novel of the Highland Clearances*, an epic historical novel of that sad time, that was a quarter-finalist in BookLife magazine's Fiction of the Year contest in 2022.

Bartlett is also the author of five nonfiction books.

Bartlett lives in a small town in Rhode Island.

For more information about the author and his books, please visit his website at:

www.jamesybartlett.com

The Hacker Golf Mystery Series

DEATH IS A TWO-STROKE PENALTY
DEATH FROM THE LADIES TEE
DEATH AT THE MEMBER-GUEST
DEATH IN A GREEN JACKET
DEATH FROM THE CLARET JUG
AN OPEN CASE OF DEATH
P.G.A. SPELLS DEATH

The last four titles are collected in a box set e-book edition titled "THE MAJORS COLLECTION"

The Swamp Yankee Mystery Series

GLITTER GIRL
COLD SECRETS
RAINBOW'S END
FAMILY AFFAIRS
RUM ROW*

** A Prequel/Novella available in e-book format only*

The Bach Musical Mystery Series

THE ORGAN JOB
THE COFFEE GARDEN
THE SONG OF ASAPH

Also available in German translation

Historical Fiction

YEAR OF THE SHEEP: A NOVEL OF THE
HIGHLAND CLEARANCES

Other titles by the author:

CADDIEWAMPUS: LOOPING FOR GOLF'S GREATS
SERPENT POINT: A POLITICAL THRILLER*
THINK LIKE A CADDIE/ PLAY LIKE A PRO
MASTERING GOLF'S TOUGHEST SHOTS

Published under the pseudonym Caleb Clarke

RAINBOW'S END
A SWAMP YANKEE MYSTERY
BOOK THREE

In this exciting new adventure, Chief of Police Gus Haddock is again chasing the Glitter Girl, Janine Stone (last seen escaping arrest at the end of Book One).

She's back in Little Penwick and causing all kinds of trouble, while Gus is also dealing with some life-changing new developments in his relationship with Maggie Wells.

Read the first chapter of James Y. Bartlett's thrilling new novel. To be notified when the book goes on sale (summer 2022) please visit www.jamesybartlett.com and join the mailing list.

RAINBOW'S END
A SWAMP YANKEE MYSTERY
BOOK THREE

CHAPTER 1

GUS HADDOCK WAS up, dressed and halfway into his morning five-mile run. It was the middle of June and the sun, even at a little after six a.m., was already climbing high in the east and had painted the Sakonnet River—which Gus could see now and then off to the left as he ran—a bright and cheerful blue. Gus ran almost every day, both to keep up his fighting trim, even though it had been more than a year since he resigned from the U.S. Army Rangers squadron in the Middle East, and to reduce some of the stress he felt now that he was chief of police in Little Penwick, Rhode Island, the smallest town in the smallest state in the Union.

He wore navy running shorts and a green Rangers T-shirt and the only indication that he was the chief of police was the radio unit he wore—the receiver clipped onto the elastic band on the shorts he wore and the handset unit flopping around on his back, attached to the collar of his T-shirt. In the year and change he had been chief of police here in his hometown, his morning runs had never been interrupted by a call on the radio from Dottie Adams in dispatch. But Gus Haddock believed in being prepared, so he carried his rig with him as he ran.

His five-mile run took him roughly forty-five minutes at an easy pace. He didn't have a time he had to beat, as he had in the Rangers, so he set an easy pace on the mostly flat roads that skirted along the broad tidal river that didn't so much flow into the Atlantic Ocean as simply existed as an extension of it. At this time of day, when the seagulls were just beginning their daily search for food among the rocks and beaches, there weren't any humans about. Which was another reason why Gus liked to run early in the mornings. It was quiet, it was peaceful and there weren't any people around asking Gus Haddock to solve their problems. Unlike the rest of the day.

The pace of life in Little Penwick had picked up since the Memorial Day weekend signaled the beginning of the summer season. That meant the population of the small town was expanded by three or four thousand new residents as the Summer Trade came back to open their beach cottages and mansions, sweeping out the winter dust and cobwebs, washing down the windows and decks, putting out the cushions on the Adirondack chairs, making sure the propane tanks on the grill were refilled and getting the golf clubs and tennis rackets out of storage, ready for a brand new season of fun in the sun.

It had only been a few weeks since Memorial Day, but Gus had already noted a slight uptick in the number of cases of DUI. That happened every year, too, as the summer trade residents came to town thinking that now they were temporarily living in a new town, that they could do anything they wanted and get away with it. This happened every year, until Chief Haddock's small police department had cited four or five drivers for being under the influence. Once the word got out that the local cops were enforcing the drunk driving laws, especially near the usual places like the Roadhouse restaurant and bar, the country club late at night and the dining club down at Penwick Point, the summer trade would pull themselves together and behave themselves. For the most part.

Although Gus Haddock went running to relieve his stress and tension, he couldn't help thinking about some of his current problems at the police department. He needed to start the process of recruiting and hiring two new officers. Two of his older officers, Carl Lincoln and Jamie McMaster, had told Gus they were moving on at the end of summer. McMaster had been hired to join the force in Fall River, a small and grimy mill city on the Taunton River just across the Massachusetts state line. Gus understood: the Little Penwick Police Department was a good stepping stone, a first job for someone looking for a career in law enforcement. A good next step would be a few years working in Fall River, where the population was larger and the ethnic make-up much different, so that the amount and kinds of crimes were much different from rural and bucolic Little Penwick. Officers working in Fall River with its more diverse ethnic make-up, would have regular encounters with violent crime, domestic abuse, car theft, vandalism and graffiti and more. And with a larger, denser population came more automobile crashes, emergency medical calls and other demands for police responses that kept someone busy throughout the shift.

Carl Lincoln, his other departing officer, was going back to school. He wanted to get his Masters degree in law enforcement, which would put him in position to hire on to a new police force as a commanding officer or a detective. He was probably looking to join the Providence department, which was large enough and funded enough to be able to hire all kinds of upper level staff.

Gus reached the tall Indian Post rock sitting just off the road, which was his turn-around point. The reddish basalt monolith, left behind millenia ago when the seas receded and the land was riven with volcanic eruptions and covered in glacial ice, had probably been called the Indian Trading Post Rock by the early settlers in this area. It made sense that the newcomers wanted to trade with the indigenous people, here the Wampanoag tribe, and they likely agreed to meet at the tall red rock near the river. Hence, the Indian Trading Post Rock, which, over time, was shortened into the Indian Post Rock.

Now heading back south, Gus picked up his pace aiming to do the last two and a half miles in a little more than fourteen minutes. He was running on the Indian Hill Road which was a quiet street with just a handful of large homes and farms. There had been just a handful of cars overtaking him during his run, so he could stay in the middle of the road. One of those cars had approached him from the south, the direction he was now running, so he saw it coming and veered over to the verge of the road. He waved as it passed. He put his head down and concentrated on keeping his speed at a steady pace, increasing it slightly when he crested a hill and started down the other side.

He was making good time, legs pumping, breathing holding steady, feeling good. Which is why he didn't notice the car coming up on him from behind. Until some primordial part of his brain heard the slight acceleration, or the soft squeal of the tires on the pavement, or maybe felt the vacuum of air sucked away by the approach of the three thousand pound collection of metal and glass and plastic.

Whatever it was, it triggered a response in Gus' brain and somehow he managed to glance quickly over his shoulder to see the bumper and left panel of the car bearing down at him. He leaped sideways and twisted and managed to avoid, at the last possible second, the front edge of the car. The driver's side mirror caught him on the upper arm and send him flying off the road and into a shallow ditch built to siphon off rainwater from the road. He fell, hard, against the wall of the ditch, taking the brunt of it on his ribcage. The force of the fall took all the wind out of his lungs.

He lay there in the ditch, tall grasses tickling his face, stunned, for several minutes. He was not sure how long. He quickly began gasping for air to replace that which had been forced out of his lungs, and when he could breathe again, he rolled over and took inventory.

His ribs ached. He suspected one or two might be broken. His left arm hurt where the mirror had struck it, but Gus didn't think it was broken. His left knee, on the other hand, was sending out frantic bulletins of pain. Gus looked down and could see a dark gray rock in the ditch and knew that his knee had collided with it. He began moving his other limbs and raised his head and decided nothing else was broken. He felt like he had been run over by a truck, but he knew he had been extremely lucky to have evaded the worst of what might have happened to him.

It was several minutes before he could ignore the spasms of pain in his knee and ribs to first pull himself into a sitting position, and then, finally, to stand upright. The car that had tried to run into him was long gone. Indian Hill Road was empty, blissfully quiet in the warm June morning, sunlight dappling the surface of the street. Birds were singing in the trees overhead, blissfully unaware of the man in the ditch.

Gus Haddock gathered himself and began walking … limping … back towards his home.